THE EXTRACTOR

THE EXTRACTOR

THE EXTRACTOR SERIES BOOK 1

MIKE RYAN

WWW.MIKERYANBOOKS.COM

Copyright © 2020 by Mike Ryan

All rights reserved.

No part of this book may be reproduced in any form or by any electronic or mechanical means, including information storage and retrieval systems, without written permission from the author, except for the use of brief quotations in a book review.

Cover Design: The Cover Collection

1

Bridge was too busy ducking bullets to think anything about the case was strange or anything other than what he was told it was. But it seemed like an awful lot of security around a residence that was supposed to be a pretty easy extraction. The home of the man in question was supposed to be that of a business man in Venezuela. The man had supposedly kidnapped the wife of an American, though the woman was originally from Venezuela and previously had a relationship with her captor. Bridge's client was a wealthy and powerful man, someone who wouldn't appreciate him coming back without his wife.

Luke Bridge was a gun-for-hire. He only worked for good causes though. Those who had something nefarious or illegal in mind need not apply for his services. A former CIA agent, he was well-versed in all forms of combat, and had been stationed all over the world. If there was a situation that couldn't, or wouldn't, be handled by the authorities, Bridge was the man for the job. Even current members of the CIA, FBI, and other government agencies would recommend him to people if the situation warranted his involvement. He wasn't cheap, though he never let the ability to pay determine whether he would take a case. His salary was usually just a means to discover how serious people were in hiring him. There were certain times when he didn't even take a dime from his clients if they really couldn't afford him.

Bridge was called The Extractor, a moniker he didn't like at first, but really had come to love and grown accustomed to. His main focus really was on helping people he believed needed it. People who would fall through the cracks if they didn't get that help. He wasn't an ex-agent who was still gung-ho on violence or still relived bad memories. Guns weren't something he was especially fond of and preferred not to use them if he didn't have to. They were just a tool for him. Luckily, they were a tool he was proficient at if the need arose. Like now.

Bridge rose up behind the cars and fired a few more rounds at his adversaries, which he now counted as being around six or seven. This wasn't a simple extraction. He had cased the house for the last few days, but didn't see a single sign of any of these meatheads hanging around. He didn't know where they came from. Unless it was the detached garage. There was a side door, but from the outside, looked like any other garage would. He certainly wouldn't have expected it to be the hangout for a bunch of thugs.

Considering his current predicament, Bridge thought about calling the whole thing off. He could just retreat, never to be seen again. But he was already there, he knew the wife was inside, if he left now, he might not ever get this close again. They would be waiting for him next time, probably with even more men than now. He surprised them this time and was still outnumbered. How could he expect to come out on top next time when there were more men waiting and expecting him?

No, Bridge couldn't back down now. He had to keep going. He had to figure out how to dispose of the men in front of him, get inside, grab the woman, then escape. He just wasn't sure how he was going to accomplish all this yet. After all, he'd already been paid twenty-thousand so far for this job. Turning around and handing it back didn't sound like such a good idea. Wouldn't do much for his reputation either, which was stellar up to this point. He wasn't about to be known as the guy who couldn't finish his jobs, took his clients money, or come back home with his tail between his legs. He was known as the best. Now was the time to prove it.

"Hey, Nic, a little help would be nice right about now."

"What, you having problems?" she replied.

"Just a few."

"Can't handle it on your own?"

"Nic?"

"OK, OK, I'm on my way."

"Thank you!"

Less than a minute later, a helicopter swooped down, getting perilously close to the house. Of course, that was Nicole's intention, to make the men nervous about the chopper, giving Bridge enough time to dispose of them. A couple of the men ran away from the cover near the house, giving Bridge a clear line of sight on them. He fired several rounds, mowing the men down. There were still four left though, not that he would have to deal with them. Nicole threw a grenade from the helicopter, landing right on target, taking care of the rest of Bridge's issue.

"Are you serious?!" Bridge yelled through his earpiece.

"What?"

"Did you really just throw a grenade?!"

"Why not? Got the job done, didn't it?"

"Jeez, Nic, we're in Venezuela, not the corn fields of Cambodia."

"You see any police coming?" Nicole replied. "Yeah, me neither."

"I would've had them."

"We don't have that kind of time to waste. Just hurry

The Extractor

up and get in there and get the woman so we can get out of here. I don't like just hovering around up here. Never know when someone's got a rocket launcher."

"OK, OK, I'm going in."

Bridge ran from the cover of his car toward the door. About halfway there, another man emerged from the side entrance of the garage and started shooting at him. Bridge saw the man and did a somersault on the ground to avoid the incoming bullets. As he got back to his feet, which was really just a squat, he returned fire, hitting the man several times and knocking him to the ground. Bridge then resumed his path to the house, reaching the front door. With him reaching the target, the helicopter rose back up into the air and hovered around the house, taking up a different position. The house was on top of a hill, with a steep ledge on the back side of it, with only a single road leading up to the front. It was the definition of secluded.

Bridge turned the handle of the front door, not that he really expected it to be unlocked. "Never hurts to try," he said to himself. He tried kicking it open, like he had done to countless other doors before, but this one wasn't opening. "Figures, this one must be reinforced."

He tried shooting the lock, hoping that would do the trick, but that didn't work any better. Bridge sighed and shook his head.

"Some days I just wish I never got out of bed."

Bridge then moved a little to the left, where the main

set of windows were that looked like they were by the living room. He then unloaded what was left of his gun into them, shattering the glass and enabling him to enter. Before going in though, Bridge put a new magazine in his gun. He removed a few lasting pieces of jagged glass by knocking them out with his gun, then crawled into the house.

Immediately after going in, Bridge extended his arms, ready for another fight if there was one to be had. Luckily nothing was there. He then heard a noise in the kitchen. Bridge slowly walked his way over there, expecting to have to use his gun in short order. He kept waiting for someone to pop their head over the countertop, but no one ever did. Once he got there, he saw a plate on top of the counter. He picked it up, then made his way to the end of the counter. He then tossed the plate with his backhand toward the other end of the kitchen, hoping to create a diversion. It worked, as a woman let out a slight scream. Bridge poked his head around the counter, seeing a woman huddled down on the floor. It was his client's wife, Maria.

"Maria."

The woman slowly turned her head and looked up at Bridge. She looked terrified with everything that had been happening.

"C'mon, I'm here to rescue you."

"You're here to what?"

"I'm here to rescue you," Bridge said. "I'm gonna

take you home. C'mon, I don't know how much time we have."

Maria sat up a little straighter, but the look on her face turned from terrified to confusion. She didn't have a clue what was going on.

"You're gonna take me home?"

"Yeah."

"I am home."

Bridge wasn't yet concerned about what was going on. He'd rescued enough kidnap victims to know that some of them were afraid of leaving due to the psychological impact of what they'd been through.

"No, it's OK," Bridge said. "It's all over now. I promise. Your husband hired me to come find you and bring you back home. So I'm just gonna take you back to him, OK?"

Maria's confused look now turned to an angry one. "No, I'm not going back."

"Excuse me?"

"I'm not going back to that man."

"Umm… I'm not sure you understand…"

"I left him because I couldn't take him anymore. He's abusive, ill-tempered, controlling, power hungry… I'm not going back to that."

"Wait, did you say you left him?"

"Of course. What else would I have done?"

It was right at that moment that Bridge knew he'd been conned. He wanted to take his own gun and knock himself over the head with it for being an idiot. He'd been suckered into taking this job. "So you weren't kidnapped?"

"Kidnapped? What? No, of course not! Who told you that?"

"Your husband hired me and told me that you had been kidnapped by your ex. I was supposed to come down here and rescue you and take you back to him."

"I'm afraid that's not going to happen, my friend," another man's voice said.

Bridge looked over to his right and saw three men walking toward him from a hallway. All of them had guns pointed at him. Bridge started backing away, pointing his gun at them as well. He tried to give them his best and most friendly smile.

"Listen, I think what we have here is a misunderstanding."

"I think what we have here is someone who has broken into my home, killed my friends, and tried to take my wife," Luis said.

He had powerful drug connections and was a dangerous man in his own right. At least Bridge could take some comfort in the fact that he wasn't breaking into the home of an innocent person. Bridge kept backing up, hoping he could by himself a little more time until he reached the sliding glass doors that led to the back of the house.

"I think what we have here is a slight misunderstanding," Bridge said. "Why don't we just let bygones be bygones? I've obviously made a mistake. I was misled with a lie from her husband…"

"I'm her husband."

"Noted. I'll explain that to her hus… former husband. I'll say she's very happy down here and everybody will be fine."

"Everybody but you," Luis said. "'Cause you'll be dead before you get to talk to anybody."

"Now what good is that gonna do? If you kill me, he'll just send somebody else to do the same thing. If you let me get out of here, I can at least explain everything to him, so he'll leave you alone from now on. I can even tell him whatever you want. You want me to tell him you guys are dead? That you moved to some other country and can't be located? Whatever you want. The bottom line is, we don't have to shoot each other. You might shoot me, but I might shoot you too, and what good is that gonna get anybody?"

"It'll give me the satisfaction of seeing you dead."

"OK, OK, I'll give you that," Bridge said. "But what if you only hit me in the shoulder and I hit you in the heart? Then you're dead and I still get to walk out of here."

"I think I'll take my chances."

Bridge could tell he was starting to run out of time. He continued walking backwards, stumbling a little as he tripped over a small piece of debris on the floor. He briefly turned his head to see what was behind him, seeing a couch. It wasn't the best piece of cover he could have gotten, but at least it was something. He then jumped over it, just as the three men started shooting at him. Luis had a pistol, but his two associates had automatic rifles. Bridge curled up on the floor behind the couch as much as he could, hoping no bullets hit any vital organs. The bullets easily ripped through the fabric of the couch.

"Nicole, I could really use your help right now!"

"Where?" she answered.

Bridge looked to his right. "Sliding glass doors to the back of the house."

"What do you need?"

"Throw everything you got through there," Bridge replied. "Just make sure you aim overtop of the couch in front of it. That's where I am! I'm pinned down."

"I am coming to save your ass again. Just hold on!"

"Not much else I can do!"

Bridge thought about trying to rise up and return fire to try and keep them at bay for a few seconds, but he figured that was suicidal. They were throwing everything at him but the kitchen sink. He wouldn't have had a chance. His only choice was to wait for Nicole, and hope that she got there pretty quick. Not even ten seconds later, a helicopter swooped in, hovering in plain view of the glass doors. Then, the doors were shot to pieces and fell to the ground as a machine gun started ripping the place to pieces.

Luis and his cohorts couldn't do anything but take cover, not having anything in their arsenal at the moment to combat a helicopter right outside the residence. Luis actually did own several rocket launchers and RPG's, but he kept them locked in a special compartment of his garage. He didn't have time to get them now.

"Luke!" Nicole shouted. "C'mon, now!"

Bridge rose up after his partner stopped firing the machine gun, peering overtop of the bullet-ridden couch, noticing everyone had taken cover. He then stood up and ran through the newly opened doorway, stopping on the balcony. The helicopter kept hovering in its spot as Bridge looked over the balcony at the very long way down. It was probably over a hundred foot drop. He was just about to ask how he was getting on there when the bullets started flying from behind him again.

"C'mon, jump!" Nicole said.

"What?! Are you crazy?"

Nicole noticed the three men start walking toward them. "C'mon, let's go! They're coming! We don't have time! Let's go!"

Bridge sighed and took a brief look behind him, observing the men coming. "I hate this."

"C'mon!"

Bridge stepped up on the ledge of the balcony, then jumped toward the helicopter, his arms hooking around the landing gear of the chopper. As soon as he was on, the helicopter quickly rose into the air. When Luis and his two men arrived on the balcony, they still kept firing at the aircraft, even though it was quickly out of range.

"Just hang on," Nicole said.

"Are you kidding me? What else can I do?"

Nicole laughed. "Hey, you're just like James Bond, right?"

Bridge mistakenly looked down, then closed his eyes. "Oh my God, I'm gonna die."

2

BRIDGE WAS SITTING outside the office building of his soon to be ex-client. It was a tall building, going up over twenty floors. Nicole was in the passenger seat of the car, trying to convince her partner that it wasn't a good idea to go inside.

"Just let it go, Luke. He already gave us the initial deposit so it's not like we're getting stiffed here."

"It's not the point."

"I know. I know you're angry about being lied to about this whole thing, but what good is going in there gonna do?"

"It'll make me feel better."

"No it won't. You just think it will. Just call him on the phone, tell him you know he lied, and fire him. It's so much simpler that way."

"But not as satisfying as looking someone in the eye."

Nicole sighed, knowing she was unlikely to get through to him. Whenever his mind was made up, it was tough swaying it. "Would you just listen to me for once?"

"I listen to you all the time."

Nicole rolled her eyes, not even bothering to touch that one. "OK, let's figure out all the things that can go wrong here."

"I've already figured them."

"He's got security, they might have guns, they might…"

"They might have to deal with me."

Nicole sighed again. "Fine, fine. If you wanna go up there and get shot up, beat up, thrown up, and every other kind of up you can think of… go right ahead."

"Thrown up? What are they gonna do, eat me?"

"Well, it sounded good at the time."

"Many things do."

"Luke, please, let's just go. We've already got twenty thousand from him. What else do you want?"

Bridge just glared at her. "You already know the answer to that. It's not about the money. It never is."

Nicole looked out the window and sighed again, making sure she was loud enough for Bridge to hear.

"Sighing loudly to voice your displeasure will get you nowhere."

"Makes me feel better."

"No it doesn't," Bridge said. "It just helps to get your feelings known."

"Same thing."

Bridge then lifted up the center console and reached inside to grab his gun. He then grabbed a magazine and put it in.

"You anticipating using that?" Nicole asked.

"Never know. But you know me… always like to be prepared for anything."

"Uh huh."

"Once I get out of the car, hop into the driver seat and wait for me."

Nicole looked confused. "Wait, you don't want me to go with you?"

"No, this is something I have to do myself."

"What, is this some macho thing you got going on? Only you can do it?"

"You know I don't care about being macho," Bridge replied. "I do care about being smart. If I have to run out of this place in a hurry, I want you already behind the wheel and ready to go. Burn rubber as they say."

"I don't like this, Luke."

"So you've said." Bridge then got out of the car. As soon as he did, Nicole slid over to the driver's seat. Bridge then knocked on the window.

Nicole rolled it down. "Yeah?"

"Just as a precaution… keep all the windows down."

"Why?"

"In case I need to jump through them. It's easier if I don't have to break the glass to get inside."

Nicole rolled her eyes and shook her head. She just

knew this was not going to end well. And she knew he knew it too. If he was already talking about jumping into car windows, keeping the car running, taking a gun with him, it meant he was expecting the worst too. But she knew it was something that Bridge wouldn't, and couldn't, let go. He could let go a lot of things, including clients who missed payments to him, or his pride and ego being bruised. But one thing he wouldn't stand for was a client who intentionally lied to him and put him in a life-threatening position because of it. It wasn't only because of the danger to him, but everyone else he worked with, mostly Nicole. But there were also helicopter pilots, tour guides, contacts, anyone who might have helped him on that assignment, their lives were also put into danger. It wasn't acceptable to him. And he needed to make sure that was known, not only to the client that hired him, but he hoped word would get out to anyone else who was even thinking of hiring him.

Bridge started walking toward the twenty story building, which housed a variety of businesses, mostly of the larger variety, including medical offices and tech companies. His current, but soon to be former client, was named Clifton Hodges. He owned one of those tech companies, which basically operated the entire twentieth floor. His net worth was in the billions and he was one of those men who liked to flaunt that wealth.

Only a few feet away from the door, Bridge saw an elderly woman who was struggling to walk. He sped up his pace so he could get to the door first and open it for her.

"Thank you, young man."

"My pleasure, ma'am," Bridge replied.

The woman slowly walked in, seemingly like she was out of breath from the strain of walking. Bridge looked at the elevator and was about to walk over to it, but his eyes went back to the woman, worrying about her condition. He then walked over to her and put his arm underneath hers so she could use it for support.

"Can I help you get to wherever you're going?" Bridge asked.

"Awe, that's very kind of you, but I can manage."

"No, no, I cannot be rejected here. I have not been in the company of a beautiful woman in months, and it would be my honor to escort you to your destination."

The woman laughed, somewhat embarrassed, then nudged Bridge on the arm. "Well aren't you the sweet talker."

"So where are we headed?"

"I don't want to take you away from your business or anything."

"Nonsense. I'm just seeing someone on the top floor in a few minutes. It's absolutely nothing that can't wait a few extra minutes."

"Well if you're sure."

"I am. I'm just gonna go up there and throw one of those rich, wealthy, knuckleheads out of a top-floor window."

The two then looked at each other and laughed, the woman assuming he was joking. Bridge wasn't as sure.

"So where are we headed?" Bridge asked again.

"Just to my doctor's office here. Luckily it's on the first floor. If I had to go any further I'd probably collapse."

"Oh, nonsense. You look like you're about ready to do a marathon after this."

After a few more minutes, they finally arrived at the office of the woman's doctor. Bridge continued to help her in, even sitting down with her in a chair after she checked in. They talked for a few more minutes, Bridge almost forgetting that he had other business to attend to.

"So are you gonna be OK from here on out?" Bridge asked.

"Oh yes, thank you very much. You're a doll."

Bridge smiled, his cheeks getting a little red. "It's been my pleasure, ma'am."

Bridge got up and started to leave, but the woman grabbed his forearm before he got away from her. "Whoever the man is that you're meeting, if he did you wrong, make sure you give him an extra shot from me."

Bridge couldn't help but laugh. He raised up his left hand, making a fist. "A left cross with your name on it."

The woman laughed as Bridge exited the office. After leaving the office, Bridge headed for the elevator. There was a younger woman standing there with a stroller and also holding a toddler. She seemed to be struggling a little, so Bridge hit the elevator button for her.

"Thanks."

"No problem," Bridge said. "Looks like you got your hands full."

"Yeah, this one just won't let me put her down."

Bridge smiled. "I understand." The elevator opened and they all went inside. "Which floor for you?"

"Oh, eleven."

"Eleven it is.

"Thank you so much."

Once the doors swung open on the eleventh floor, the woman tried juggling the child in her arms, then putting her down, which the child wanted no part of.

"Allow me?" Bridge asked, pointing towards the stroller.

"Uhh, sure, thank you."

Bridge pushed the stroller off the elevator and onto the main floor as he waited for the mother, which was only a few more seconds. Once the mother took control of everything again, Bridge stepped back on the elevator.

"Thanks for your kindness," the woman said before the doors closed.

"My pleasure."

The elevator opened a couple more times for other passengers who were getting on and off on various floors. But once it stopped at the twentieth, it was finally Bridge's stop. He got off and was immediately greeted by a receptionist sitting behind a desk.

"Can I help you?"

"I'm here to see Mr. Hodges," Bridge answered.

"Is he expecting you?"

"He'll want to see me."

"Your name?"

"Luke Bridge."

"Have a seat please."

Bridge looked to his left and saw a small waiting area that consisted of ten chairs and a coffee table with some magazines on it. It was the first time he'd been in the building. His previous encounters with Hodges were spent at a couple of different restaurants. It was an expensive looking area, with not a cheap looking finish to be found anywhere. After sitting down, Bridge looked back to the receptionist and saw her on the phone, hopefully announcing his presence. Once she put the phone down, she immediately stood up.

"Follow me please?"

Bridge quickly got up and hurried over to her, following the woman as she turned down a hallway. They turned left, then went down another hallway, the woman finally stopping as they came across Hodges office. She knocked, then opened it, allowing Bridge to go in. Upon seeing him, Hodges got up from behind his desk, a wide smile on his face after he took the cigar out of it, and eagerly walked over to Bridge to shake his hand.

"Luke, great to see you."

A half-hearted smile came over Bridge's face, knowing the man would soon change his tune after he heard what he had to say. Still, Bridge returned the man's handshake, figuring at least they could start civil.

"So did you get Maria? Where is she?"

The two walked back over to Hodges desk, both of them sitting down across from each other.

"There's kind of a funny story about that," Bridge said.

"What do you mean? I don't understand. Do you have her or not?"

"I do not."

"What? You went down there to get her. What happened?"

"I'm gonna get to the funny part. Here it is. You ready? I actually found her and was ready to leave with her."

"OK?"

"And you know what the funny part is? She didn't want to come."

"What?"

"She said she wasn't leaving to come back with you," Bridge said. "She said, she wasn't kidnapped, that you were basically abusive towards her, and she was happy where she was, with her ex, which just so happened to be a major drug dealer down there. So yeah, all things considered, I was lucky just to escape with my life."

"None of that is true of course."

"Oh, I believe all of it is true. See, you weren't there. I was. She had absolutely no interest in coming back with you. And I think you lied to me about this whole thing."

"So you're not going to bring Maria back to me?"

"Uhh, yeah, no. No, I'm gonna leave her just where she is because that's where she wanted to be."

"I need her. And I want her back."

"See, that's the problem with you rich, powerful people. You think you get to choose what other people think or do and make decisions for them. But you don't. She's a grown woman, she can make her own choices, and she has. You need to move on."

"This is ridiculous. I pay you to do a job and you come back here with nothing. You came highly recommended and all I get is excuses as to why the job isn't done."

"Mr. Hodges…"

"No, I paid you very well to go down there and find her and bring her back. I think maybe I should get some of my money back since you didn't complete the assignment."

"Well, that's gonna be another little bit of an issue," Bridge said. "See, since you lied to me, and put me in a very dangerous and unhealthy situation, I'm gonna have to bill you extra for my services."

Hodges looked at him incredulously. "Extra?"

"That's right. I'm thinking another twenty-thousand should cover it. Consider it a going away bonus."

"Bonus?" Hodges looked stunned that the man had the audacity to come at him for extra money after failing the job. "You're out of your mind if you think I'm going to give you another penny."

Bridge just smiled at him. He wasn't leaving until he received another check. "It's OK, I'll wait until you come around to your senses."

"You go down and get Maria and perhaps you'll get your bonus. Not before."

"No, see, you're not quite understanding what's happening here. I'm dropping you as a client. I don't work for you anymore. But I would like my bonus for a job well done since your deception put me and my team in danger."

"You're crazy."

"Some might think so."

"You better get out of here before I throw you out."

"I'd be happy to leave as soon as I get that extra check."

Hodges pushed a small button under his desk that basically acted as a panic alarm and alerted his security staff that there was an issue.

"This is your last chance to get out of here on your own two feet," Hodges said.

Bridge looked unconcerned. "Oh? Why? Did you push a little button to have a couple idiots in ties show up in a minute?"

Hodges smiled. "You've got an air of cockiness to you. I like that. I almost hate to throw you out of here."

Only a few seconds later, the door opened, revealing two large looking men in suits. They looked the part of the tough security detail.

"Oh, this must be the goon squad," Bridge said.

Hodges stood up from behind his desk. "Mr. Bridge, don't make this more unpleasant than it has to be. Just walk out of here."

"See, that's one of my problems. I don't always make the most rational or logical choice." Bridge finally stood up as well. "I'll give you one last chance to give me my check before I take Punch and Judy out here."

Hodges laughed. "I guess we have a standoff here."

"No. A standoff is created by two equal parties. I don't have an equal here."

Hodges had finally had enough. "Boys, take Mr. Bridge out to the curb and make sure he doesn't come back. Don't be gentle either."

The two men walked over to Bridge and grabbed him on each side of his arms, escorting him to the door. Bridge wrestled his arms free as they got to the door, putting his hands up as if to say he was surrendering.

"Boys, boys, I know when I'm licked. I'm quite capable of walking out on my own without your assistance."

"Let's go hotshot," one of the guards said, trying to grab Bridge's arm again.

Bridge successfully eluded the man's grasp, then

suddenly kicked the man between the legs, putting him down to his knees. He then turned around and forcefully kicked the other man directly on his knee, dropping him to his good one. Bridge then raised his knee, driving it into the other man's face, crushing his nose and breaking it. As the man fell onto the floor, Bridge turned back to the first guard, who was still on his knees in pain holding his man parts. Bridge then took a step back, then delivered a thrust kick to the man's head, putting him onto his back.

With the two guards down and out of commission, Bridge turned back to face Hodges. He adjusted his clothes and started walking back to the desk. Hodges' face had turned red, embarrassed by the whole episode. His guards had never failed him before. He took a puff of his cigar, hoping that would relax him.

"I'm sure we could work this out," Hodges nervously said.

"There's nothing to work out. A check will do. Now. Unless of course you have some other people you would like me to meet."

"No. No. A check." Hodges sat back down at his desk and reached for a drawer.

Bridge wouldn't have put it past the man to have a gun in the drawer, so he made sure if he did, any thoughts of using it were put out of his mind. Bridge cleared his throat and tapped his side, making sure Hodges saw what he was doing and knew the reference.

"Just in case you have ideas of reaching for something in there, know that I qualified first in my class in firearms at Langley."

Hodge didn't have a gun in the drawer, but even if he did, he wasn't dumb enough to try something that stupid. He was a smart businessman. He knew when he was licked and to throw in the towel. Losing a little bit of money wouldn't have hurt him a bit. He slowly opened the drawer, making sure he didn't make any moves that would alarm Bridge. Hodges took out his checkbook and frustratingly tossed it on the desk.

"I imagine another twenty thousand should cover it?" Hodge asked.

While that number would have satisfied Bridge before he came in, the stunt with the security guards annoyed him and raised the number. He put his finger on his chin and rubbed it.

"I dunno. I feel a little sore now that I just had a little workout."

Hodge rolled his eyes, knowing he was being flimflammed. "Twenty-five?"

"Well, I dunno, I feel like we're getting there. Maybe we should make it an even thirty."

"Thirty?"

"Yeah, it was twenty on the way in, but all this extracurricular activity… well, my time's valuable."

Hodges sighed, then started writing the check. "Thirty." After he was done, he handed the check over.

"Thank you. I would say it's been a pleasure doing business with you, but it really hasn't. Oh, and just in case you have ideas about stopping this check, or if it bounces, I will be back. And I'll be in a much worse mood."

"It'll be good."

"Glad to hear it."

"You know, Mr. Bridge, I'm a powerful man. You don't want to make me an enemy."

"Same could be said for me. Because if I ever see you or your men again, my friends in the FBI might be interested in investigating some of your activities if you know what I mean. And we sure wouldn't want that to happen, would we?"

Hodges sat there, giving Bridge the evil stare, knowing that he was being bested.

"I thought not," Bridge said. "So let's just let bygones be bygones and agree that we never need to see each other again."

Hodges gave a slight nod of his head, not really liking the fact that he was going to have to let Bridge skirt on this. But he knew Bridge had contacts with several law enforcement agencies and wasn't willing to jeopardize any illegal activities he had going on with an investigation.

"Enjoy the rest of your day, Mr. Bridge."

"Oh, I will."

Bridge then got up and walked out of the office, stepping over the fallen men on the floor as he did. He calmly walked down the hall until he got into the elevator, not a care or concern in the world. He knew Hodges wasn't dumb enough to send anyone else after him. He knew Bridge had beat him.

Once Bridge had left the building, he immediately located the car and walked over to it. Nicole had been anxiously on the lookout for him, and noticing his calm demeanor, assumed everything was OK. When Bridge got in the passenger seat, he immediately handed the check over.

"Looks like we need to go to the bank. Told you he'd play nice."

Nicole looked at the check. "Thirty thousand? How'd you manage that?"

"Oh, it was a bit of a back and forth negotiation."

"He give you a hard time?"

"Nothing I couldn't handle and wasn't ready for."

"I didn't hear any gunshots and nobody was running from the building, so I guess it went pretty smooth?"

Bridge looked at her and smiled. "Easy as pie."

3

Nicole barged into the hotel room and immediately headed for the bedroom. She already knew what she was going to find though. It was the usual culprit when Bridge didn't answer her messages. It almost always meant another woman.

Nicole stopped in front of the closed bedroom door and put her ear up to it. She couldn't hear anything. It was still early in the morning though. It actually worked out better if they were still sleeping, she thought. It was always better when she surprised them. At least in her mind. She got a little bit of a kick out of it. It was either always make a joke out of it or shoot them out of anger. And she loved Bridge too much for that.

The door swung wide open, and Nicole stormed in, looking at the bed and seeing Bridge and his lady cohort sleeping under the covers. The sheets went up to their shoulders and Nicole could see that neither of them had tops on. She could only assume the rest of their bodies matched in their lack of clothing. They were snuggled together, with Bridge having his arms around his lady friend, her back rubbed up against his chest.

Ignoring the bed momentarily, Nicole walked over to the window and threw open the curtains, letting the bright morning light shine into the room. The light shined down on the occupants of the bed, hitting them in the face, causing them to stir around. Nicole loudly cleared her throat to help make her presence known. Bridge and the woman started to wake up, each of them opening their eyes. Bridge put his arm up over his eyes to shield them from the light.

"What's going on?" Bridge groggily said.

"Time to rise and shine!" Nicole happily replied.

"What?"

"What's going on babe?" the woman in bed asked.

Bridge wiped the sleep from his eyes and was able to clearly see Nicole standing by the window. He could only grin at her, knowing what she was doing. Bridge and the woman sat up in bed, her holding the sheets up over her chest to cover herself.

"Hey, who are you?" the woman asked. She then looked at her partner from the previous night. "Who's this woman standing here? Why's she here?"

"Oh, her?" Bridge replied.

"I'm his wife," Nicole calmly answered.

"His wife?! He never said anything about his wife."

"Oh he didn't, huh?"

"No!" The woman, offended at having been lied to, turned to Bridge and slapped him hard across the face. "How dare you!"

Nicole smiled, thinking this was working out even better than she had hoped. She put her hand over her mouth to prevent her from laughing. The woman in bed, still holding the sheets over her naked body, stormed off the bed and picked up her clothes off the floor. She left the bedroom, choosing to get dressed in the main room. Bridge, still having a grin on his face, watched the woman leave. He continued to sit there, only one remaining sheet covering his lower half. He just looked at his partner, finding it slightly amusing. Bridge didn't get out of bed until he heard the main door slam shut. That was his cue.

"Should I turn around?" Nicole asked.

"Does it matter? I mean, we are married and all, right?"

Nicole couldn't help but laugh. "True, true."

Bridge put his feet on the floor, Nicole taking every opportunity to examine the body of his six-foot frame before he covered it up with pants and a shirt. He then went over to the dresser and grabbed a bottle of water.

"Enjoying yourself?" Bridge asked.

Nicole shrugged, her facial expression indicating that she was. "I must say, it worked out so much better this time. The last one you shacked up with took it much too nicely."

Bridge rubbed the side of his face. "It was the slap that did it?"

"Oh yeah. She seemed like a real feisty one."

"She was. How'd you get in anyway?"

"Oh, I just told one of the housekeepers that I was your wife and I left my key card inside."

"Why do you get such pleasure out of doing this?" Bridge asked.

"I don't know. Why do you get such pleasure out of sleeping around with strange women?"

Bridge went over to the edge of the bed and sat down. He raised one of his eyebrows at her. "You really need or want an answer to that question?"

"What's wrong with me?"

Bridge rolled his eyes, not wanting to have this discussion again. They seemed to have it every other month. "For the thousandth time, Nicole, there's nothing wrong with you."

"Then what's wrong with you?"

"There's nothing wrong with me either."

"Then why can't we?"

"Because we're friends, we're business partners, and a relationship between us would never work. It never does in these kinds of…"

"These kinds of what?" Nicole asked.

"These kinds of… you know. Whatever we are. I don't know, you know what I'm saying."

"Why can't we just try?"

"Because if it doesn't work, then our friendship

goes, you'll probably go to, then our business relationship dies, then I'm out a partner, and then I have to find someone new to do what you do, and that takes a lot of time to work out the kinks, not to mention trust, and you know I don't trust people all that much."

"Why do you just automatically assume it would fail?"

"Because you know me," Bridge replied. "My relationships never work."

"Because you never try. All you ever do is go to some bar and find some floozy to go back to your hotel room with you."

"Because I'm not a relationship type of guy."

"You're just afraid of commitment."

"I'm afraid of ruining what we already have."

"But we don't have anything," Nicole said.

"Not true. We have a very lovely friendship, where we can tell each other anything, a very profitable business, where we make a lot of money and help people. Why would you wanna chance all that?"

"Because there's more to life than just business."

Bridge let his head fall into his hands, not believing he got sucked into this again. He sighed, thinking it felt like this was going to last a while. He really did love Nicole, and if they were in any other type of business, he'd probably want that relationship with her as much as she did with him. But they weren't in any other type of business. He was an ex-CIA agent with trust issues, used to being on his own, lived in a hotel, and their work took him all over the world and placed him in dangerous situations. He was known as The Extractor. When things or money were lost, people disappeared or were put in bad spots, Bridge was the man they called. Usually after all other hope was lost or the police or other people investigating came up empty.

Nicole was Bridge's partner, and no matter what, he didn't think he could do the things he did without her. She was usually the point person, making the initial contact with potential clients, weeding people out, determining who really did need their help. She was also a computer specialist, also having worked at the CIA as an analyst, not to mention accompanying Bridge on missions, giving him whatever tactical support he needed. Bridge couldn't picture another person ever filling her shoes. They just couldn't. She was invaluable, indispensable, irreplaceable, and everything else one could imagine that was wrapped up in one pretty package.

Nicole was all of five-foot-five, but knew how to handle herself, was an excellent shot, and saved Bridge's bacon more times than he could count by now. That's why these discussions were always so difficult for Bridge. He'd seen several husband and wife teams over the years and things always ended badly for them. Sometimes they let their love for each other come before business, a couple times resulting in the loss of one of their lives. There were two other couples he knew of that wound up hating each other and got divorced. Bridge didn't want something like that to happen to him and Nicole. He cared too much about her to risk getting in deeper with her.

It was one of the reasons he went around with different women. He wanted to keep up with the appearance that he wasn't interested in a relationship with Nicole. He couldn't say it wasn't fun meeting new women sometimes, but it wasn't as nice as he made it out to be. It didn't really matter what the reasons were, though, at least not at that moment. Now he just had to find a way out of the conversation.

"Hey, why'd you bust in here anyway? I assume it wasn't just to chase another strange woman away?"

"Why not?" Nicole asked. "It is kinda fun."

"And something you're getting far too used to. How many's that make this month?"

"Only three. But who's counting?"

Bridge rolled his eyes. "Only three."

"Well each time I had something to discuss with you and you weren't answering your phone."

"Because I was in bed sleeping. People do that you know."

"Yes, but each time was because you were up too late fraternizing with the opposite sex, which made you sleep in too long."

"I can't win."

"Plus, business before pleasure, right?"

"So the saying goes," Bridge replied.

"If you had left your phone on, or answered it, then I wouldn't have to barge in. Would I?"

"Or you could be like most normal people and just leave a message and wait for that person to respond back."

"Where's the fun in that? Besides, business is pressing. And like you always say, the sooner we get in on something, the better it is for us to find what we're looking for. Right?"

"I hate it when you use my own words against me."

Nicole just gave him a delightful looking smile. "Just one of my many, many talents."

"So I take it we have a new job?"

"We do."

"What's this one about?" Bridge asked.

"A helicopter went missing."

"A helicopter? The entire thing?"

"Yep."

"Where at? Hopefully off Long Island, or Massachusetts, or maybe even Vermont. Don't tell me we gotta travel to another country or anything."

"It's Mexico."

Bridge tilted his head back and looked up at the ceiling, letting out a loud sigh. "Don't say it."

"Mexico."

"Really? Why'd you have to do that?"

"Gotta go where the clients are, Luke."

"You know, we just got back from that other thing

and I was hoping to spend a little time here before shuffling off again to another part of the world."

"It's not another part of the world, it's just south of the border."

"You know what I mean. Mexico, really? Why couldn't it go missing off Florida or something."

"Because the people were vacationing in Mexico."

"People? Who is missing?"

"Just one. A man named…"

Bridge put his index finger in the air to stop his partner from continuing. "Wait, wait, I don't wanna hear about anything yet. Let me eat breakfast first, take a shower, get refreshed."

Nicole looked to the bed and pretended like she was sniffing something. "Yeah, it does have kind of a musty odor over there."

"Don't start, Nicole."

"I'm just saying."

Nicole then walked over to the bed and picked up the sheet with her index finger and thumb, looking like she was afraid to even touch it. A nasty face came over her like she was looking at something gross.

"It's not gonna bite you," Bridge said.

"How do you know?" Nicole continued lifting the sheets up, thinking she saw something. She then lifted up an article of clothing, which appeared to be a woman's thong. "Ewww. Gross."

Bridge got a wide smile on his face. "Should I return that later?"

"Sure, if you don't mind getting the other side of your face slapped. I'll just trash it."

"Kind of you." Bridge took his shirt back off then went into the bathroom and got the water running. "You mind calling me up some room service?"

"You really need to eat and shower before talking about this?"

"A person should never discuss business feeling dirty and on an empty stomach."

"You need some help in there?"

"Nicole!"

"All right, all right, I was just asking."

Bridge stuck his head out of the bathroom door. "Order yourself something while you're at it."

"Gee, thanks so much for thinking of me."

"You know me, I do what I can."

"Uh huh."

"Hey."

"What?"

"Is it really Mexico?" Bridge asked, hoping she was just playing some kind of cruel joke on him.

"It's really Mexico."

Bridge grunted and closed the door to take his shower. "Mexico. Can't wait."

4

By the time Bridge got out of the shower, Nicole was already sitting at a table eating breakfast. Once he got fully dressed, he walked into the main room and saw her eating eggs, french toast, and bacon. From the looks of her plate, she was pretty hungry.

Bridge threw his arms in the air. "What, you couldn't wait for me? You had to start without me?"

"I was hungry."

Bridge sat down and started eating. He then looked at both of their plates and realized they had the same thing. "Oh, look, twinsies. We even have the same meal. Some might think that was planned."

"Can I help it if we like the same thing?"

"So, about this job, what are we looking at?"

"Vacationing family, went to Mexico, husband went on one of those helicopter tours, helicopter never came back."

"Wow, that was enlightening," Bridge said. "Told me so much. A few more details would be nice."

Nicole grinned and crinkled her nose at him. She had a file folder on the desk that she opened up. "Bill and Mary Hower, very wealthy couple, live here in New York, went on vacation two weeks ago in Mexico with their two children, who are ten and twelve years old."

"Doing good so far."

"Bill went on one of those helicopter rides while his wife and two children went to town shopping and sightseeing. Bill never came back."

"You just went from Bill going on a helicopter ride to never coming back to here and now a couple of weeks later, I'm sure a bunch of stuff happened in between there."

"To be perfectly honest, not a whole lot."

Bridge put a piece of bacon in his mouth and just kept it there like he was smoking a cigarette. He found it hard to believe not much happened between those two points. "Really?"

"What do you want me to tell you? Should I just make some stuff up to make it more helpful?"

"Might not be more helpful but it sure would sound better."

"Yeah, well, can't really help you there. But, basically, after Bill went missing, Mary contacted the Mexican authorities, who promptly came up with nothing. She then contacted the FBI, who, from what I can tell with my sources in the bureau, have also come up with nothing."

"What do you mean, nothing?" Bridge asked. "Nobody's come up with anything?"

"That's what I said."

"I'm assuming since you're coming to me with this that the helicopter didn't crash?"

"That's a good assumption."

"Why? Why not?"

"Because no wreckage has been found," Nicole replied. "Like I said, it was a helicopter tour ride, it took the same route every day. They've searched the route, not a single sign of a crash or wreckage."

"Well then it's obviously a kidnapping. Waiting for a ransom call."

"No call has ever come in."

"That you know of."

"Luke, there's been no ransom demand. After two weeks, one's not coming."

"You're right. A ransom call would've come in within a day or two."

"So the question is, who took him and why?"

"No, that's the second question," Bridge said. "The first question, is he still alive? If the answer to that is yes, then it becomes who took him and why? Then the next question becomes what do they want with him? It's obviously not his money."

"Unless they need him to get even more money."

"Possibly. What does Mr. Hower do?"

"He and his wife own a business consulting firm. Know what it's called?"

"Don't tell me."

"Hower and Hower Consulting."

Bridge tilted his head up. "I told you not to tell me."

"Why?"

"Because I just knew it was going to be something like that. Hower and Hower Consulting. Why do all business and consulting firms sound so… business-like?"

"Maybe because that's the *business* they're in. Get it?"

"That's so not funny. But seriously, why don't they ever dress it up a little, make it something fun, catchy, like… Consultants R Us or something?"

"Ooooh, real catchy," Nicole replied. "Fun too."

"You know what I'm saying.

"Maybe it's because they're bringing these *business* people in to fix your *business* and not to coordinate some office party?"

"Huh. Maybe… nah, that makes too much sense. So I take it we've been hired by Mrs. Hower?"

"Uh huh." Nicole slid the file across the table as Bridge finished up his breakfast.

"How'd she latch on to us?"

"Our friends in the FBI."

"Oh, how nice of them to bring us business."

"Yeah. They recommended us."

"Are they not still investigating?" Bridge asked.

"Umm, apparently it's one of those kinda, maybe, a little bit, sort of deals."

"Oh, just love those. So they don't have anything and are already moving on to something else basically is what you're telling me."

"That's mostly it. They were on it, but haven't come up with anything. From what I understand they have no other leads."

"When all else fails, bring it to us."

"At least we'll get paid for this job."

"You know it's not about the money."

"Yeah, well, the last time I checked, hotels aren't free. Especially this one."

"True."

"And considering the last five jobs we worked, we only got paid for three of them, and that barely even paid for this place."

"It's not about the money, Nic, it's about helping those who need it. And they can't always afford to pay."

"But it's nice to sometimes get clients who can."

"So when are we going down to Mexico to meet Mrs. Hower?"

"We're not. She's already here."

"What?"

"She's been back in the states for a week now."

"Wait, so her husband has disappeared in Mexico, and she's back here like nothing ever happened? Somebody has a strained marriage."

"I don't think it's quite that simple. They went down

for an extended weekend getaway. But the kids had to be back in school so they couldn't stay down there. Mary wanted to be home with the kids to try and keep things as normal as possible."

"Still, I'm just saying, if I was married…"

"There's a nice thought."

Bridge mockingly smiled at her. "Funny. No, but if I was married, and my wife went missing somewhere, I sure as hell wouldn't leave until I found out what happened. Nothing would be able to tear me away."

"Not even your kids? I mean, if you had any."

"I might take them back home, have them try to get back to a normal routine, but I sure wouldn't give up looking."

"She's not giving up. That's why she's coming to us."

"Maybe. I'm just saying, if it was me, I'd have my parents, relatives, whoever I could get to stay with them, I'd have them stay with them, and then I'd head back to wherever it was until I came back with my spouse."

"You're also an ex-CIA agent, trained in combat, investigating, disappearing, things like that. You're comfortable in doing that sort of thing. Not everyone is."

"Even if I wasn't, I'd do it anyway."

"Well, as soon as you're done stuffing your face, we can go talk to her."

"What do you mean, stuffing my face? You were

done before me. How much are we getting out of this job, anyway?"

"We didn't talk specific numbers," Nicole answered. "She did say money wasn't an issue though."

"Well then what are we waiting for? Let's get this show on the road."

They took a few extra minutes to get themselves together, then headed for the door. Just as they were about to leave, there was a loud knock. The two stood there looking at each other, neither making a move to answer it. They just let whoever it was continue knocking for a minute.

"Are you expecting someone?" Nicole asked.

"Nope. Are you?"

"Uhh, this is your residence, not mine."

"Oh yeah. Well, I figured since you're here so often, I mean, you practically live here and all..."

"Don't tempt me." The knocking continued. "Well aren't you gonna answer it?"

"Do I have to?"

Nicole rolled her eyes and then opened the door, finding CIA agent Eric Happ standing there. Happ was a good friend of both of theirs, and was actually the agent that referred Mrs. Hower to them. He was also a good source of information and didn't mind sharing it. He didn't care about red tape, though he never crossed the line in revealing secretive information that would get him into trouble. Well, most of the time. He was mostly interested in just getting the job done and helping people. Same as Bridge and Nicole.

"Hey, Happ," Bridge greeted. "Happy, Happy-Happster, Happmeister…"

Happ briefly looked up at the ceiling, not really enjoying the word games Bridge usually played with his name. He couldn't say it really irritated him either. It was just one of those things he put up with. "You done now?"

"Uhh, yeah, I think I ran out."

"Good. Let's talk about the Hower's."

"Oh, wait, got one more…"

"Really?"

"Yeah… uhh, nope, yeah, it's gone, inspiration left me. Sorry."

"I think we'll all survive."

"I'd invite you in for breakfast but we just finished," Bridge said.

Happ took the liberty of going in anyway. "I already ate this morning anyway."

"So what brings you to this neck of the woods?"

Happ sat down in a chair, soon followed by his friends directly across from him on the sofa. "Your next case. I'm assuming you're doing the Hower job?"

"Well, I just learned of it myself a little while ago. We were about to go talk to the missus and see what's up."

"I wanted to give you some info about it."

"Nicole already filled me in."

"Not about everything," Happ said. "There's something weird about this case."

"Well, a missing helicopter will do that."

"No, it's something else."

"Were you working this?"

"No, some other agents had it. They've come up empty."

"Did they actually go down there and investigate?" Bridge asked.

"No. Couldn't. The Mexican government doesn't want any official inquiries going on down there, not until there's something concrete to go on. If we get there, they might be willing to let a small team go down there and extract Hower if he's still alive."

"You mean a black ops team?"

"Yeah. If there's a credible link that we can find. We haven't found it yet. We're trying to piece things together, but there's not a lot to go on."

"And there's been no ransom demands, communication with the wife, anything?"

"Nothing."

"So it's not a kidnapping," Bridge said.

"At least not one they want money from. It's always possible they kidnapped him and killed him."

"Why? What would that get the people that took him?"

"Who knows?" Happ said. "Maybe they just wanted to make a statement."

"But there hasn't been any statements, has there?"

"No."

"And if that was the case, the helicopter would have reappeared by now, wouldn't it?"

"Yeah."

"Maybe the thing just crashed," Bridge said.

"There's no evidence anywhere of a crash. We've looked at satellite footage, we had a drone go up there to look for wreckage, nothing."

"So what's this about then?" Bridge studied the look on Happ's face. It seemed like there was something he wasn't saying. He was holding back. "What is it? What is it that you're not saying?"

Happ shook his head. "Nothing."

"Don't tell me that. I've known you long enough to know better."

"It's just that umm… well, you know about Mexico and missing persons."

Bridge nodded. "Yeah."

Nicole looked at the two of them. "What? What am I missing?"

Happ knew the numbers off the top of his head. "According to the Interior Ministry database, there are at least thirty-seven thousand missing persons in Mexico. And that's likely a conservative estimate. It's probably closer to fifty."

Bridge scratched his face, not looking too happy. He already knew the statistics. Nicole, though, wasn't as well-versed in the numbers.

"That's terrible," she said. "How can there be so many?"

Happ just looked at Bridge, waving his hand at him, letting him do the explaining if he wanted.

"Because it's a corrupt country," Bridge answered. "Between organized crime, corrupt police forces, corrupt politicians, it's a wonder anyone lives there peacefully."

"But how can they just let so many people fall through the cracks?"

"Because they don't look for them. They don't investigate."

"Investigations lead to things being uncovered that they don't want discovered," Happ said. "Half the time the people investigating are the ones that did the crime to begin with. Or were involved by looking the other way. It's a broken system."

"It needs to be cleaned up."

"That's not our job," Bridge said. "That's their problem. Our job will be in finding Hower. Has there been any press coverage on this?"

"No," Happ answered. "Not a word."

"Strange. A wealthy American goes missing in Mexico and nobody knows about it?"

"The family immediately contacted the American Embassy in Mexico. The CIA was also contacted a few days later when it was apparent that the investigation was going nowhere."

"The CIA's moving on?"

"No. But like I said, with no leads, there's nothing else for us to do. If we knew where he was, we'd go in and extract him. But there's nothing to extract yet."

"That's where I come in," Bridge said. "Boots on the ground."

"Basically. And the family's willing to pay for someone to go in there and find out where he is."

"It's not gonna be easy."

"No one said it would be."

Bridge got up and walked around for a minute, thinking about everything. Now it was Happ's turn to read his friend's face, able to tell there was something else on his mind.

"What's the problem?" Happ asked.

Bridge stopped walking around as he answered. "We're talking about this like it's an active situation."

"It is."

"I mean like he's active. It's been two weeks, there's no ransom, let's stop pussyfooting around and dancing around the subject. There's a very real possibility, and probably even the likeliest scenario, that Bill Hower is dead."

Happ and Nicole both looked at the floor, not wanting to think about that possibility, even if they both knew he might have been right.

"But we don't know that," Happ said. "And until we have confirmation of that, we have to go under the assumption that he's still alive."

"For what purpose?" Bridge asked. "Why would

someone keep him alive? The only reason kidnappers don't use someone for a ransom is if they have specific skills they're looking for. That doesn't seem to apply in Hower's case."

"Maybe not." Happ then got up and walked over to him. "Your job isn't to reason things out though."

"My job is to stay alive while investigating dangerous situations."

"Your job is to find him. One way or the other. If he's alive, bring him back. If he's dead, at least the family will know and have closure. Just find out which one."

"Well as long as it's easy."

Happ grinned. "If it was easy, it wouldn't be coming to you."

5

BRIDGE AND NICOLE were on their way to Mary Hower's house, a good forty-five minute drive from the hotel. It gave them plenty of time to talk about the case before they arrived at their client's home.

"You really think he's dead, don't you?" Nicole asked. "I could tell by the way you were talking. It wasn't you just bringing it up or anything. You really believe it."

"Doesn't matter what I think or believe. It only matters what I can prove, you know that."

Right now, all they had to go on was theories and guesswork though. Without really digging into the situation and figuring out what was going on, that's all they could talk about. Hopefully they could get more by talking to Mrs. Hower, but it didn't sound like she knew much more than anyone else.

"You know what really bothers me?" Bridge asked.

"What?"

"They go down on vacation, right?"

"Yeah."

"And right away, the husband goes off on his own in a completely different direction than his family."

"So?"

"You don't think that's strange? I mean, don't most families, when they go on vacation, do things together? He just sends his wife and kids to the city so he can go on some helicopter sightseeing tour?"

"I guess when you think about it it does seem kind of odd."

"Why wouldn't he go with his wife and kids?"

"Maybe he didn't like to go shopping?"

"But in the file I read that they'd been down in Mexico before, right?"

Nicole was in the passenger seat with the file in her hand. She opened it up again to read it. "Uhh, yeah, looks like they'd been down there several times before. Seems like it was an annual trip or something. Says they were down there once a year for the last five years."

"So what's he need to go touring on a helicopter for?"

"Maybe it's something he always wanted to do."

"Or maybe he was doing something he didn't want his wife and kids around for."

"I think you're grasping for straws."

"Maybe," Bridge said. "But sometimes you reach

for something and actually get what you're reaching for."

"And sometimes you get ten pounds of air."

"Yeah, well, we'll see."

They continued throwing wild theories into the air during their drive until they finally reached the Hower house. It was in the suburbs and upon pulling up in the driveway, Bridge and Nicole looked over the three thousand square foot home.

"Nice," Nicole said.

"Yeah, it's OK."

"You're right. It's no beautiful hotel room or anything, but, I guess some people could live here."

"Wisecracks will get you nowhere."

"I mean, I know I could never live in a place like this. Way too nice and comfy. I'd much prefer a cold, unpleasant, dirty hotel room."

"Hey, there's nothing dirty or cold about it."

"Why is it again that you won't consider moving out of that place?"

"Why would I? I have all the comforts of home there."

"But it's not actually, you know, a home."

"Listen, with our work, we're gone half the time anyway," Bridge said. "If I bought a house, what would I have to do? Clean, wash dishes, do laundry, mow the lawn, trim hedges, rake leaves, wash windows, maybe clean up dog doo if I were to get a pet or something, right? Now, why would I wanna put myself through all that aggravation?"

"Because it makes you happy?"

Bridge laughed, then slapped his knee. "Ha. Happy. That's a good one. See, with a hotel room, I don't have to do any of that stuff."

"I guess you have a point."

"It pains you to say that, doesn't it?"

"A little bit."

"Besides, since I stay there year round, they give me a discount on the rates."

"But even with a discounted rate, I'm sure it can't be enough to be financially more viable than just owning a house, or even renting an apartment, and just having a cleaning person come in once a week, even while you're gone."

"But then I gotta pay someone else to do that," Bridge said. "Plus, owning a house ties me down to one spot for thirty years."

"Not if you sell it."

"Well, doing it this way, if I don't like the new management, or the hotel staff, or I don't like the way the cleaning crew shampoos the rug, I can just switch to a different hotel. Simple. Just the way I like it."

"You have an answer for everything."

"I try."

"Or more like an excuse."

Bridge smiled. "One person says tomato, another

says tomahto. Now, can we stop with the grill-job and go in and see our new client?"

"Let's get the ball rolling."

They got out of the car and walked up the expensive looking brick walkway. Before they even got to the door it suddenly opened.

"Now that's what I call service," Nicole said.

"Yeah. Almost like they knew we were coming."

As they walked up to the door, they noticed a middle-aged woman standing there, waiting for them. She was about five-foot-seven, thin, wearing an expensive looking dress, and had short black hair with a few streaks of grey in the back. The worried expression on her face told Bridge that maybe some of his preconceived notions were not correct.

"Mrs. Hower?" Bridge said.

"Yes. You are Mr. Bridge?"

Bridge almost cringed, though he was careful not to show it in front of someone who already seemed upset. He hated being called Mister. "Just call me Luke. Mister makes me feel like I'm my father or something."

"Of course."

"This is my assistant Nicole."

"Would you both please come in?"

Mrs. Hower held the door open for her guests to enter. Once inside, she led them into the living room. It was a big room, complete with expensive looking paintings and a piano. As Bridge sat down, he nonchalantly looked around at his surroundings.

"You play?" Bridge asked, extending his arm toward the piano.

Mrs. Hower looked over at it and smiled. "Oh, no, my children get weekly lessons."

It was always tough for Bridge to start an unpleasant conversation with a client. He hated just being blunt and immediately getting into things. It always seemed so crass and unfriendly. But unfortunately, there were usually no easy ways to break into those conversations.

"So, we obviously know that your husband is missing," Bridge said. "Can you tell us what made him fly on a helicopter while you went into town?"

"Uhh, it was just something he always wanted to do. We've obviously flown quite often, but always on airplanes. He'd never been on a helicopter before and it was something he was interested in."

"And you've been to Mexico before, right?"

"Yes. We've gone down there for the last five years. We've never had any issues before."

"What made your husband pick that helicopter? Anything specific?"

"Umm, honestly, I don't know," Hower replied. "He didn't mention much about it. He just told me the night before that he was finally going to go on one, and that if I took the kids into the city, that once he was done, he would meet us there. So I said OK and that was it."

"Have you guys had any problems or issues with anybody, either on a personal or business level?"

Hower shook her head. "No, no one."

"No unhappy clients that maybe have threatened revenge or getting even or anything?"

"No. We generally always have happy clients. In the event that one is not satisfied with something we always go the extra mile to fix whatever the issue is. We make sure no one is ever left unhappy with our services."

"What about personal life? Any issues with anyone? Neighbors, school, people from your past, anyone?"

"No, we've always tried to be nice, kind, get along with everyone."

"So there's not a single enemy that you can think of?"

"Nobody."

"What about money?" Bridge asked. "Any money problems? Bad investments, business deals, gambling, anything like that?"

"No, money is not an issue. We're pretty well off."

Bridge looked at his partner, wanting to sigh and throw his hands up, though he was careful not to do anything that would look like he was discouraged with Mrs. Hower right there. He gave Nicole sort of a head nod, hoping she would pick up on the clue and ask the next question. Luckily she did. Bridge hated asking the next set of questions. It always seemed better coming from Nicole.

"Mrs. Hower, we're gonna have to ask some unpleasant things to get a better understanding of things," Nicole said. "We're not accusing or making anything personal."

"I understand. Ask what you need to."

"Were there any problems in your marriage? Infidelity, talk of divorce, anything along those lines?"

Mrs. Hower let out a smile, not offended by the questioning. She assumed it was coming at some point. "No, we've got a good marriage. Like anyone, we've had our share of fights or disagreements, but nothing out of the ordinary or anything. We've always shared the same values in regards to us, raising the kids, things like that. Divorce was never something either of us ever talked about. We've got a good marriage."

Bridge lowered his head slightly, then ran his hand over it. They weren't getting anything by being there. According to the wife, everything was just perfect. And it was always possible that that was actually the case and she wasn't lying, but it sure didn't help them any if it were true. All it did was make finding the real reason more difficult.

"I'm sorry, I know I'm not helping much," Mrs. Hower said.

"It's fine," Nicole replied. "We just need to make sure we get everything down so we can try to narrow things down."

"I understand."

"What about Mexico?" Bridge asked. "Any issues down there? Even something small? Argument with a vendor, stopped by a police officer, disagreement with a hotel worker?"

Mrs. Hower thought for a minute, then shook her

head. She couldn't remember a single incident or problem in the last few years they'd been down there. "No, I'm sorry. Nothing comes to mind."

Bridge had trouble believing they didn't have a single incident or problem anywhere. It sounded like they had a perfect life, and he knew there was no such thing. Everyone had problems somewhere along the line, and sometimes they hid them from their partners. He had a feeling this was going to be one of those times, when the wife was the last to know.

"Well, I think that'll pretty much do it for now," Bridge said, slapping both of his knees.

"OK, well if there's anything else I can do…"

"There is actually one more thing."

"OK?"

"Bank statements. If you could supply bank statements for the last year, that would be most helpful."

"Why? What would you be looking for?"

Bridge smiled. "I don't know. Inconsistencies mostly. Things that are out of place. Something that you might not notice as unusual but someone with no ties would." Bridge could tell that Mrs. Hower looked unsure in giving him their financial records and sought to reassure her how important it was. "I know most people tend to balk at requests like that, but it is very important that we can safely say that this is not money related and move on to something else. That's all that matters."

Mrs. Hower briefly thought about it, then relented.

The Extractor

"You're right. Give me an hour or two to get everything together, then I'll send it to you."

Bridge reached inside his pants pocket and removed a business card. He then handed it to his client. "You'll find everything you need on there. Phone number, email, address. Email me when you get everything together."

"I will. Can you tell me when you will go down there looking for him?"

"The sooner we can go through these bank records will help. After that, it'll probably take two or three days to get everything coordinated, supplies, accommodations, figuring out a plan of attack down there, so hopefully no later than three days from now."

Bridge and Nicole spent another twenty minutes asking their client questions, hoping they'd get at least one answer that would throw some better light on the situation, not that they were expecting much at that point. They weren't thrown for a loop as nothing else that was said would help to explain what happened.

"Well, I guess that'll do it for now," Bridge said, standing up. "We're gonna start working on some things. If there's anything else we need, we'll contact you."

"Will you please keep me updated with everything?" Mrs. Hower asked. "Even if you don't have anything new to report. It would help to relieve… you know."

"I absolutely will. Probably every few days, OK?"

"Thank you. Oh, and before you go, I have something for you." She got up and walked over to a desk and opened the drawer. She removed a small piece of paper, then returned to her guests and handed it over to Bridge.

Bridge looked at it, not used to getting paid before starting the job. "This is very generous, ma'am. Thank you."

"If you need more, just let me know."

"This should be fine."

"I'll have another one waiting for you when you bring my husband home."

Bridge just looked at her, trying to give a warm smile, even if he wasn't sure he could live up to the deal. "I'll do my best."

Bridge and Nicole then left the house. As they walked back to the car, Nicole snatched the check out of his hand.

"Twenty thousand," she said. "Nice down payment."

Bridge didn't sound as enthused. "Yeah."

"Why so glum?"

"Because I don't like anything about this case. I don't like where it is, don't like anything I've heard, don't like that we have no leads, don't like anything."

"Well, you know they don't give us the easy ones."

"Just once I'd like a cupcake assignment."

"Cupcake assignments come up with cupcake money."

"I'd be fine with that. Just once. That's all I ask. Just one time."

"You know you'd miss the challenge."

The two of them got back in the car and just sat there for a few minutes. Nicole finally broke the silence.

"So what do you think?"

"I think this case stinks," Bridge said.

"I know that. But anything else?"

"I almost hate to say it, but I think it sounds like Mrs. Hower is living in some kind of fairy tale. They have no issues or problems anywhere. That's not normal."

"Maybe they really don't though."

"I dunno, I don't believe it. I refuse to believe there are people out there who have no problems whatsoever. It's just not natural."

"It is possible you know."

"I call hogwash."

Nicole then started the car and pulled out of the driveway. "Back to the hotel?"

"No. Let's head to the bank first and deposit this before it bounces or something."

"You really think she'd do that?"

"You know our history with checks?" Bridge asked.

Nicole looked at him. "You're right. Bank first."

"Then we go back to the hotel. Hopefully we'll find some small speck of dirt that can springboard us somewhere… anywhere. I don't even care where at this point. Just give us something."

6

Mrs. Hower had emailed Bridge their bank statements for the past year. Bridge and Nicole were sitting at the kitchen table of his hotel room as they looked the statements over. They had been going through them for the last hour, trying to find something that stood out. The problem with going through records like this was that they didn't know what they were looking for. It was always easier, and faster, if they had a specific thing that they hoped to find.

"You really had to do a year, didn't you?" Nicole asked. "You couldn't have done three months? I'd even have settled for six."

"The problem with that is if Mr. Hower was planning his own disappearance, he most likely would have been planning for a long time. Usually a person would do that for longer than three or six months."

"You think he planned his own disappearance? That

he just dropped off the grid, left his wife and children? For what? Why?"

"I didn't say that. I just said *if* he was planning his own disappearance. At this point of time, I'm making no guesses. He could've flown the coop, been kidnapped, been killed, or any combination of those."

"You know, I was thinking…"

"Stop that, it's dangerous," Bridge said with a smirk.

"Ha ha, very funny."

"I thought so."

"Anyway, I was thinking, instead of always rushing to the bank with a check that we hope clears, why don't we just scan the check using one of those apps."

"What apps?"

"I don't know, can't you do that with the bank app?"

"I don't know, can you?"

"I don't know. I think we should look into it."

"OK. I authorize you to look into it."

"You authorize me to look into it?" Nicole asked.

"I do. Thanks for volunteering."

Nicole's shoulders slumped and she sighed. "Why do I always get suckered into doing these kinds of things?"

"Because you're better at it than I am."

"It doesn't take a whole lot of skill."

"You're just better at the small detail type of things," Bridge said.

"You mean you just don't like doing the small things so you get me to do them."

Not wanting to talk about his idiosyncrasies, Bridge quickly changed the subject. "So have you found anything that looks promising yet."

"There you go, always changing the subject when it's something you don't want to talk about."

"I did not."

"Yes you did. You always change the subject when it comes close to a criticism of you or something you don't want to discuss."

"I don't do that."

"Oh really?"

"Yes, really. I would have no problems discussing any of this stuff with you, except we're on an extremely time-sensitive case right now, and there's probably where we should be putting our entire focus on."

Nicole rolled her eyes, knowing he was doing it again, using the crutch of the case to avoid discussing anything else.

"So have you found anything or not?" Bridge asked.

"Not yet. I'm only through three months though. There's a lot of transactions here."

"Nothing abnormal?"

"All just regular stuff. You find anything?"

"If I did, you really think I'd be asking you?"

"I have a feeling this is going to be a waste of time," Nicole said.

"It's not a waste of time if we can eliminate things."

"Well one thing's for sure, they don't have money problems."

They continued poring over the bank statements for the next several hours, carefully checking each transaction, no matter how innocent it seemed. They made note of any transactions that weren't clear, so they could investigate and cross reference any similarities. Once they were done eliminating the simple transactions that could easily be explained, such as bills, shopping trips to the supermarket or other similar stores, they then moved on to the items they couldn't quite as easily identify.

Nicole had taken the first six months, while Bridge had the most recent six months, and after they were finished, they started checking each other's lists. After getting to the third month on Nicole's list, Bridge stopped, thinking something looked familiar. There was a transaction on there that he'd seen before.

"Wait a minute," Bridge said, grabbing his list too so he could compare.

"You got something?"

"I don't know."

"Well you must think you have something."

"Could be."

"Feel like sharing?"

Bridge then pointed to the transaction in question. "It's this one here. It was on my list twice."

"Well if you keep going down you'll see it's on mine two more times."

"Five times total."

"And it's all money going out," Nicole said.

"And each payment is exactly two thousand dollars."

"Each one is exactly one month apart too. The fifteenth of every month."

"There's quite a few coincidences right there. Let's find out where this is going to."

Nicole was already on the computer typing and had the answer by the time he was finished talking. "The routing number comes back to a bank in Mexico."

"Mexico. The coincidences keep on coming."

"We're gonna need some clarification from Mrs. Hower on what these transactions are."

"Before we do that, let's see if we can find any others."

They continued going over their respective lists, though they didn't find anything else that interested them nearly as much. Once they were done with their list, they switched, wanting to be thorough and make sure nothing got by them. Bridge grabbed his phone on the table and called Mrs. Hower to see if she had an explanation. After a brief greeting by both parties, Bridge didn't waste time in getting down to business.

"We've gone over the bank records and we did come across something strange, something that stood out to us."

"Oh, what was that?" Mrs. Hower asked.

"There were five withdrawals from your account for five months in a row, ending last month. Each transaction, the amount was two thousand dollars, and each time was on the fifteenth of every month."

Mrs. Hower didn't reply.

"Mrs. Hower?"

"Oh, yes, I'm here."

"Do you have any idea what these withdrawals are for or who they're to?"

"Uhh, no, I'm afraid I don't have any idea."

"Were you aware of these transactions?"

"Well, I don't always look over the bank statements too closely. Usually Bill does all that."

"So you didn't notice two thousand dollars leaving your bank account every month?"

"Mr. Bridge, we have a big mortgage, several cars, two boats, a vacation home, pool service, lawn service, investments, charity givings… me noticing two thousand dollars is missing in any given month is hardly a big reveal. That's like someone noticing a few quarters is missing out of their change drawer. It's just not something I would pay much attention to."

"Did your husband mention anything about these payments?"

"He did not. I imagine they must have been for our trip."

"Wouldn't that be a little unusual?" Bridge asked. "Why would he make five equal payments? And what would be so expensive?"

"Well, we stay in an expensive hotel while we're

there, we do a lot of activities. We don't just stay in our hotel room."

"That would still be unusual, don't you think? As you said, people of your means don't need to budget things out and make payments. You could pay for everything all at once when you got there, no?

"I don't know. I guess he wanted to spread things out."

"Could be. I just thought it was slightly unusual and wanted to mention it."

"Have you found anything else that seemed out of the ordinary?"

"Uhh, no, not really," Bridge said. "That was the main thing."

"So you think these payments were not for our trip?"

"I don't really think anything at the moment. I just don't have enough information. It certainly could turn out that way."

"Or it couldn't."

"Or it couldn't," Bridge repeated. "But it's too soon to tell."

"Please let me know if you find something else."

"I will."

After getting off the phone, Bridge sighed and tossed his phone down, picking up the bank statements again. Nicole didn't need to be told how it went based on what she picked up from their conversation.

"Didn't know anything about it, huh?"

Bridge shook his head. "She did not. I get the feeling she rarely even looks at the bank statements."

"There's quite a few people who don't. Especially people who don't have to watch every penny coming in or going out."

"I guess. Maybe we should get this bank account number over to Eric and see if he can come up with anything."

Nicole cleared her throat, faking a cough. "Ahem! What do you think I'm here for?"

"Looks?"

"I am a computer specialist you know. I did spend several years in the CIA analyzing things, looking things up, finding things, researching things…"

"That's a whole lot of things."

"It is. So I think I'm pretty capable of finding this out on my own without help."

Bridge put his hands up, thinking he'd hit a sore spot. "No problem. Just thought I'd mention it in case it was a little over your head or you thought you needed some extra help."

"Over my head? Really?"

Bridge smiled, realizing he hit a sore spot. He knew she was perfectly capable of finding the information they needed, but couldn't resist teasing her a little. She would do the same to him. He kind of liked it when she got a little feisty. Made her even more attractive to him, even though he wouldn't act on that appeal.

"So you gonna get on that?" Bridge asked.

"For your information, I'm already on that!"

"Oh, OK. So you're already on the ball then?"

"Yes, I'm on the ball," Nicole replied, angrily striking the keys on her laptop.

"If you don't calm yourself you might need a new laptop."

"If you don't calm yourself you might need a new assistant."

"Oh, I couldn't have that."

"Then maybe you should shut it."

Bridge put his fingers on his lips and pretended to zipper them. "Consider them shut."

"It's about time."

"So how long's that gonna take you, give or take?"

"A few minutes. Aren't your lips supposed to be shut?"

"OK, OK, just get back to me when you find out what you're looking for."

Nicole put her fist into the air at him. "Oh, you'll be the first to know."

7

While Nicole was running down the information they needed, Bridge went to the refrigerator and pulled out a soda. It was his usual beverage of choice when he was working on something. He avoided alcohol whenever he was on a case, as he didn't want anything to impair his mind or judgment. He walked back in the room, popping the tab of the can, and putting it on the table. As soon as he put it down, Nicole picked it up and started drinking it.

"Thanks. How'd you know I wanted one without me even saying anything? I love how we know each other so well we can read our minds now."

Bridge sighed and rolled his eyes. He just shook his head and smiled. "No problem." He then walked back to the refrigerator to get another soda, this time for him. He came back over to the table, this time keeping the can firmly in his hands, though he wouldn't have been surprised if she reached up and wrestled it away from him, just to annoy him.

"I've got it," Nicole said.

"What?"

She put her hands up. "The information about the mysterious bank account."

"Oh. Good." Bridge then sat down and started looking at the screen. "So what are we looking at?"

"The account belongs to a man named Ricardo Rodriguez."

"Who's he?"

"I don't know, I haven't gotten that far."

"So what do you have then?"

"A name. Which is more than we had five minutes ago."

"Oh. I guess so."

"So now I'll look Rodriguez up and see what I can find on him."

"OK, while you're doing that, I'll check in with Mrs. Hower again and see if she recognizes the name."

"What do you think the odds of that'll be?" Nicole asked, thinking it was a waste of time.

"Probably not high, but hey, they even find a needle in a haystack once in a while, right?"

"They do?"

"Well I'm sure somebody must've found one at some point through the ages."

Bridge grabbed his phone again and started pacing around the room as he called Mrs. Hower.

The Extractor

"Mr. Bridge, I didn't expect to hear from you again so soon."

Bridge laughed. "Yeah, that makes two of us."

"Find something else."

"Well, yeah, we found the name of the account that those weird transactions belong to."

"Oh?"

"Do you know a Ricardo Rodriguez?"

"Ricardo Rodriguez… no, I don't believe so. Why?"

"Well he's the man the account belongs to."

"I don't recall the name, I'm sorry."

"Did I tell you that the account comes back to a bank in Mexico?" Bridge asked.

"Uhh, no, I don't believe you did."

"Does that ring any bells perhaps? Someone you and your husband knew down there?"

Mrs. Hower was silent for a few moments as she thought. Knowing she was trying to remember, Bridge tried to help her out, wanting her to go as far back as she could.

"Think back to all the previous trips you've made there," Bridge said. "It doesn't even have to be this last one. Maybe someone you just knew by their first name or last name, or a nickname, anything that might have any similarities to Ricardo Rodriguez."

Mrs. Hower continued thinking, and after a good solid minute that felt like ten, she came up with something. "Wait, when we were down there last year, my husband left the room. I think it was in the morning or early afternoon, I'm not really sure of the time. Anyway, after a while I came down with the kids and I saw him in front of the hotel talking to someone. I asked him who it was and he told me the man's name was Ricky."

"Did he say what the man did or what he was talking to him for?"

"Said he was a local tour guide who was just looking to get some business or something."

"Hmm, could be the same guy. Do you remember what he looked like?"

"Umm, no, not really. I didn't get a close look at him or anything. I really only saw him from a distance."

"How did your husband seem after talking to him? Nervous, rattled, normal, different?"

"Uhh, he seemed a little different now that you mention it. Almost like he was over anxious about something. After I asked him about it, it was like he wanted to quickly change the subject."

"And did you ever see the same guy before or since then?"

"No, not that I can recall."

"OK, well that should be good enough anyway."

"You think he might be the same person as the bank account?"

"Well, they might be," Bridge answered. "But it might not be too. Either way it gives us something to look into."

After hanging up, Bridge relayed the information to Nicole, not that it would be of much help. They wouldn't get much by the name Ricky, who probably wasn't a tour guide if he was actually the one Bill Hower was making payments to. Nicole was still busy typing away on the computer, trying to find out who Ricardo Rodriguez was.

"How are you making out?" Bridge asked.

"Might take a while."

"Why's that?"

"You know how many Ricardo Rodriguez's there are?"

"Just reverse trace him back from the bank."

"What do you think I'm doing?"

Bridge shrugged. "I dunno. Beats me. Playing solitaire?"

Nicole briefly glared at him.

"Without getting an evil death stare, since the task is so daunting, should I call Eric and see if he can help?" Bridge asked.

"I guess two heads are better than one."

"You mean three."

"No, I don't really count you."

"Oh."

"Eric might have contacts in the Mexican government who might know who Rodriguez is too, especially if he's on a wanted list."

Bridge laughed, thinking of the reverse. "Rodriguez might have contacts in the Mexican government who alert him that we're looking for him too."

"Why are you so pessimistic?"

"I'm not being pessimistic."

"Yes you are."

"No I'm not."

"Well you're certainly not being optimistic."

"I'm being realistic," Bridge replied.

"Oh. So that's what you call it?"

"That's what I call it."

"I call it being negative and thinking the worst already."

"It's just calling it like it is."

"Speaking of calling, stop flapping your gums and call Eric already."

"Oh. Yeah."

Bridge grabbed his phone again and called Happ, explaining the situation to him and what they'd found out so far. Happ said he'd start looking into it and that he'd call them later if he got anything. While they waited for their FBI contact and friend to get back to them, they continued digging on their own. A few hours went by without Bridge and Nicole having much luck.

"I thought you said you were supposed to be good," Bridge said, knowing full well what type of response he'd get back.

Nicole stopped typing and slowly turned her head to look at him, giving him a look that could kill a lesser man. "You wanna say that again?"

Bridge laughed. "Nope. I don't have a death wish."

"Are you sure? 'Cause it kind of sounds like you do."

"Nope. Not me."

The two stopped working for a little bit so they could eat dinner, but got right back to work as soon as they were done. About twenty minutes after picking up again, there was a knock on the door.

"You wanna get that?" Bridge asked.

Nicole stopped typing again as she looked at him. "Why do I have to get it? It's your room."

"It's just Eric."

Nicole scrunched her face together, unsure how he came to that conclusion. Happ hadn't called back as far as she knew to tell them he was coming.

"Eric? How do you know that?"

"It's his knock," Bridge replied.

"His knock? You can identify people by their knock?"

"Yeah. You mean you can't?"

"Uhh, no, I've never tried to put any extra thought into trying to figure out who was knocking at the door. I've always figured it was easier to just look out and see who it was. Or, you know... open it."

"That's the easy way out. Things are much more interesting when you can figure out who it is without having to get up. What if you're busy and it's someone you don't want to talk to? Then you won't be angry and tearing yourself away from something important just to find out it's someone you're not going to open the door for anyway."

"It's amazing how your mind works sometimes."

"I agree."

Nicole shook her head, not intending it as a compliment. She finally slapped her hands down on the table, realizing that Bridge was not going to get up, seeing as he was just sitting there looking at his computer.

"It's all right, I'll get it."

Bridge took his eyes off the screen as she walked over to the door. "Oh, gee, thanks. I appreciate it."

Nicole continued shaking her head as she got to the door. She looked out the peephole and saw it was Happ, making her sigh, not wanting Bridge to have the satisfaction of being right. She opened the door in a displeased fashion, yanking it open.

"Come on in, Eric."

Happ slowly walked in, hearing some anger in her voice, thinking maybe he had come at a bad time. "Should I go out and come back in again?"

Bridge laughed. "No, come on in, Eric. She's just mad because I knew it was you without looking."

"You did?"

"He can apparently identify people by their knocks now," Nicole sarcastically said.

"You can?"

"Yeah," Bridge answered. "Makes it more fun, don't you think?"

"Uhh, yeah, I guess. Can't say I've ever tried it myself."

"See, everytime you come here, you knock three times. Never two, never four. Always three. And you do it in the same exact way every time. It's mid-level, not too forceful, but not soft either, and almost always the same amount of time between each knock."

Nicole and Happ just looked at each other, neither one ever hearing of something so ludicrous.

"You're telling me you actually count the amount of time between each of his knocks?" Nicole asked.

"Well, it's not like I time it or anything," Bridge replied. "It's a basic estimate that I'm pretty confident in."

"Do you do this for everyone?" Happ wondered.

"Uhh, yeah, pretty much. Like I was telling her, it makes it more convenient when you're busy and don't want to open the door for someone you're either avoiding or don't like."

"I see."

"Let's not get into that again," Nicole said.

"So what brings you over?" Bridge asked.

Happ had some file folders and papers in his hand and brought them over to the table where he sat down across from his friends. "This brings me over. Your problem."

"My problem? I don't have a problem. I'm just…"

"Yeah, yeah, we know," Nicole interrupted. "It's the Hower's problem, you're just the one investigating. Can we get on with it?"

Bridge leaned over the table and whispered. "She's a little touchy today."

"Whisper about me again and you'll see how touchy I can get."

Happ put his hand over his mouth to conceal his laugh. He always found it amusing how the two of them bantered back and forth. "Anyway, regardless of whose problem it is, I'm here because of Ricardo Rodriguez, you know, the person you asked me about."

"You found something?"

Happ nodded. "I did. And it isn't good."

"Oh, good," Bridge said, rubbing his hands together, probably taking more delight in it than he should have. "Wait, not good as in he's not good, or not good as in you didn't find much worth talking about?"

Nicole rolled her eyes. "He just said he found something. Would he have said that if he came up with nothing? Why don't you try listening better?"

Bridge sat back again, putting his hands up as if he were fearful of her yelling at him again. "OK, OK, carry on."

Happ opened the folder and started taking some papers out. He passed them to his friends so they could read for themselves as he recited the contents from his memory. "Ricardo Rodriguez... an independent operator down in Mexico, no affiliation to one gang or cartel over another, he pretty much works for whoever pays him the most money."

"A drug runner?" Bridge asked.

"Ehh, no, not really. I mean, he'll do it from time to time if the money is right, but it's not a specialty or anything. He will literally do any job for anybody for the right amount of money."

"If he'll do anything for anybody, he must run afoul of the cartels from time to time though, no?"

"Well that's the thing, most of his work is for the cartels in one fashion or another. He won't cross them. But he'll work for any of them."

"That's unusual, isn't it? Don't they like for their employees to be loyal to them and no one else?"

Happ gave a shrug. "I guess he's built up some trust or something over the years, I don't know. All I know is what's in the file."

"I don't notice anything major in here," Nicole said, flipping through the pages. "Like, it doesn't seem like he's a hard-time type of guy."

"He's probably participated in knocking off a few guys, either directly or indirectly. He's more the type that will set you up to be knocked off, then slip off into the bathroom when the hitman comes along to take out who he brought with him."

"Then comes out of the bathroom and fixes his tie when the shooting stops like nothing's happened," Bridge said.

"Exactly."

"So what would Bill Hower be doing messing around with a guy like this?" Nicole asked.

"That's the million dollar question," Bridge replied.

"Have a million dollar answer?"

"I don't even have a five dollar answer."

"Well, I hate to say it," Happ said.

"Then don't. Every time someone says they hate to say something, they come right out and say it anyway. Every time. Never fails."

Happ smiled. His friend was right. He was going to say it anyway. "As I was going to say, I don't think you're gonna find the answers here. The only place you're going to find the answers is in Mexico."

Bridge didn't reply. He simply stared at the wall for a minute, the others noticing his lack of attention.

"Something wrong?" Nicole asked.

Bridge sighed. "It's just this Rodriguez guy."

"What about him?"

"If we go down there and talk to him, and he's affiliated with gangs down there, are we setting ourselves up for a bigger problem?"

"I think as long as you don't go down there and roust him you should be fine," Happ said.

"You think?"

"Well, I can't guarantee it."

"But if I don't go down there and jack him around a bit and threaten him he's not gonna tell us anything."

"Guess you do have a problem after all then, don't you?"

"I certainly do."

8

Bridge and Nicole had just grabbed their luggage after their plane arrived at the Mexico City International Airport. They rented a car and then went to their hotel and checked in. They only got one room, making sure it had two beds in it. Bridge wasn't comfortable with the two of them splitting up for any reason. At least not until they were sure what they were dealing with. As they put their things away, Nicole looked out the window of their tenth floor room, staring out into the city.

"Seems like such a beautiful city," Nicole said.

"You'll change your mind once you get a couple of guns staring at you in the face."

"You know, you keep making remarks like that, ever since you found out we'd be coming here. What exactly is your issue with this place?"

"My issue is that it's an extremely corrupt and dangerous place."

"Seems like you could say that about just about anyplace."

"Maybe," Bridge replied. "Sometimes your fears are unfounded and sometimes they're true. In this case, they're true."

"Something happened to you here, didn't it?"

Bridge put a couple of his shirts in a drawer. "I guess you could say that."

"What was it? Or is it top-secret?"

"We don't live by those top-secret orders anymore, remember?"

"Just giving you an easy out if you wanted it. So what happened?"

Bridge thought about it for a few seconds, thinking about whether he wanted to tell her, or if he really wanted to relive it. He finally decided to come out with it, since it wasn't anything deeply personal or anything. It was just a job. A job on which he got double-crossed. But he still remembered it like it was yesterday.

"I was working with the agency at the time, probably a year or two before I met you. We were tracking some illegal arms dealers, found them here in Mexico, but of course, we decided to let the authorities know first. And you know what that meant? Working hand in hand with some higher-ups in the Mexican government. You know what that also meant? Getting betrayed."

"How?"

"We were down here for about two weeks, getting pretty much nowhere. We knew the guy was here, just couldn't pin him down anywhere. Got a few tips, a couple that came close to nailing him, but he just kept slipping away. And we couldn't figure how he was doing it."

"He had help."

"Inside help," Bridge said. "A lot of it. It turned out that two of the people in the government we were working with, that were supposed to be helping us and guiding us through some of the rougher areas and people, were actually on the guy's payroll. That's how he was always slipping out from under us."

"How'd you figure it out?"

"I was actually down here with another agent. There were the two of us. We got a tip that the guy we were looking for had some type of studio on the top floor of some apartment building. He was using it as an office or something to conduct business. We rolled on it, and informed our contacts in the Mexican government. By the time we got there, they knew we were coming. We got ambushed, my CIA partner was killed, and our Mexican friends turned on me and tried to take me out at the same time."

"Were you hurt?"

"No, amazingly enough. I somehow managed to escape without a scratch. I killed the two Mexican government officials though."

"What about the guy you were after?"

Bridge sighed, feeling like it was a blemish on his record. "Slipped away. Never got another line on him again after that."

"So the guy's still out here roaming around? Maybe if things break our way, you can get your sights on him again. Finish off an old score."

Bridge shook his head, as nice of a thought as it was. "No, unfortunately not… well, I guess it is fortunate that he's not still around since he's a bad guy and can't hurt anyone else, but he's dead now anyway."

"Oh. What happened? Do you know?"

"Yeah, he got taken out by a rival gang a few years ago. So he's long dead and gone now."

Nicole nodded, now understanding his disdain for being there. "So that's why you've hated coming down here. Bad memories."

"Yeah, pretty much."

"But that's not everyone here. I'm sure not everyone in the government is on the take."

"No, but that's the problem. You just don't know who is. If you can't trust the people you've got to go to to make things happen… you're swimming up the creek without a paddle."

"But that's still just the government. It's not the people. I'm sure there's a lot of fine people down here."

"It's not about the civilians," Bridge said. "The normal, everyday, regular people here, on average, are about the same as they are in any other country. They're hardworking, devoted to their families, and just wanna make a good life for themselves. But there's a lot of bad things that can go on here if you don't know what you're doing."

"Maybe we just need to find one of those hard-working people who can give us a hand?"

Bridge shook his head. "Not here. Even if they know anything, they won't tell us. There's too much retribution that goes on. If you know something and tell, you earmarked the rest of your family for death. It's unlikely anyone's gonna tell us anything, at least directly. We'll have to use some creative lines of questioning to get any answers we're looking for."

"So why are we staying here then?" Nicole asked, looking around the room. "I mean, it's a really nice place, but if we know Rodriguez was hanging around that other hotel, why didn't we just book a room there?"

"Never ask questions about people in the same hotel that you're sleeping in. You have a tendency to get unwelcomed visitors. Plus, people tend to clam up if they know the person you're asking about is a regular there. It's bad for business."

"So if no one here is gonna help us, and there's no one we can trust, how are we going to find any answers?"

Bridge grinned. "Like I said, we'll have to get creative."

"That doesn't sound at all dangerous" Nicole paused for a second before continuing. "OK, it sounds totally dangerous. Like, locking us in a room with twenty bad guys dangerous."

Bridge continued smiling. "We'll see."

"Can I just go rent another helicopter and sit up there with a missile launcher until you're done?"

"Already told you, Nic, I want you spending most of your time here on the computer, trying to find out some more leads with whatever information I hand you. I'll do most of the work in the field."

"I'm not gonna get to see any of the town?"

"We're here on business, not a sightseeing tour. You can go to Cancun or something next month if we have nothing going on."

"You're gonna keep me chained to a desk the entire time we're here? Doesn't sound so bad under certain circumstances."

"Get your mind out of the gutter and focus on what we're here for."

"All work and no play makes Luke a dull boy."

"It also keeps Luke an alive boy," Bridge replied. "Besides, I can play once we get back to New York."

"Promise?"

"Uhh, yeah, no, uhh, not with you."

Nicole frowned. "Can I get that missile launcher now?"

"No!"

9

BRIDGE WAS near the airfield that the helicopter that Bill Hower used was once located. There was a small building on the property that was still being used, mostly by other operators. Bridge saw the signs of three other businesses that looked like they all used the same building. He went inside and was immediately greeted by a middle-aged, grey moustached man behind the counter.

"Good morning, sir, what can we help you with today? Would you like a helicopter ride?"

Bridge smiled and reached into his pocket. "Yes, actually, I have the cards for one of your helicopters here." He put down the name and number of the pilot of the Hower helicopter, which he simply copied down after a quick internet search. "I was talking to this guy, oh, maybe a year or so ago when I was down here last, about taking one of his sightseeing tours. Told him I'd be sure to use him when I came down again. So… I'm ready and rarin' to go."

The smile on the employees face quickly evaporated once he looked down at the card. "Oh, I'm sorry sir, that operation is no longer in service here."

"What? No kidding?"

"Yes, but I'd be more than happy to have you go up in another helicopter. We have a couple standing by right now."

"Oh, OK. That should be fine. What happened to the other guy though? He said he'd be here for a while. He just pack up and move to a new spot or something?"

"Uhh, no, unfortunately there was an accident or something a few weeks ago."

"You mean he crashed?"

"Well that is the prevailing opinion, but most of us think otherwise."

"Really? What do you think happened?"

"He was having a lot of money problems and he mentioned to one of the other pilots that he had a loan that he was having problems keeping up with."

"Oh, you mean a bank?" Bridge asked. "Maybe they were going to repossess his chopper or something so he vanished."

"Well, I believe the loan he had was with some less than reputable individuals."

"Ooooh." Bridge put his elbows on the desk and leaned forward, looking around to make sure no one else was there listening, even though he knew there wasn't. He then whispered. "You mean like gangsters or cartel members or something?"

The clerk lifted one of his hands off the desk. "That's the rumor."

Bridge stood straight up again and nodded his head. "Ahh, I see." He then started shaking his head, not wanting to give off the impression that he was actually there digging for information. He just wanted to seem like a regular tourist. "That's a shame. When I met him before, he seemed like such a nice guy. Shame if he got mixed up with the wrong crowd, you know?"

"Yes, everyone here got along with him well. But such is life, right?"

"Yeah, I guess so. So tell me, since I'm not from around here, how would someone go about disappearing like that? Where would he go? How would you hide that chopper of his?"

"There are many things that could be done. Fly to a different country, set it down in a remote part of the country and leave it behind, paint it a different color to disguise the look of it, any of those things."

"Oh, I see."

"Should I set you up with another helicopter now?"

"Uhh, yeah, that's fine." As the clerk walked away from the desk to set his customer up with a flight, Bridge faked remembering something, slapping himself in the head. "Oooh, wait a minute."

The clerk immediately looked over at him, thinking something was wrong. "Is everything OK, sir?"

"I just remembered something. I think I remember seeing or reading something about that. Was there an American on the chopper with him when he disappeared?"

"Uhh, yes, there was."

"That's right," Bridge said, slapping his hand down on the desk. "I do remember seeing something about that now. Whatever happened to that guy? Do you know?"

"Unfortunately no one knows about him either. It is assumed that he crashed and died as well."

"But what about the people that think the pilot vanished?"

"Well the passenger was a wealthy American, perhaps they made some type of deal to aid in his escape."

"Oh, like paying off the debt or something?"

The clerk shrugged. "Anything is possible I suppose. Why all the interest?"

"Well, I was interested in going up, but now...." Bridge shook his head for emphasis, making it seem like he was having second thoughts about flying.

"I promise you, sir, it is most safe."

"I dunno. I mean, what if I go up in one of those choppers and I wind up disappearing too or something. I kind of got the heebie jeebies now."

"The what?"

Bridge held his hand out and started shaking it. "A little nervous now."

"Oh, I promise you, sir, you have nothing to worry about. What happened was a once in a lifetime incident."

"I dunno, are you sure?"

"You have my word. I personally guarantee it. You will come back here after your flight safe and sound. Absolutely nothing to worry about."

"You're sure? 'Cause I got a wife and kids back at the hotel waiting for me to come back."

"I give you my word. And... I'll take twenty dollars off your bill as a courtesy to persuade you that you are in good hands."

Bridge smiled. "Well, all right. I'll take you at your word."

"Excellent. You will not be sorry. You will see. You'll have the time of your life up there."

"I hope so."

∼

Bridge got back to the hotel and immediately went to the room. He was a little surprised to see that it was empty though. He scoured the whole room, then the main floor, wondering what had happened to Nicole. He tried calling her cell phone, but she didn't pick up. After waiting for close to an hour, Nicole finally came back to the room, a couple of bags in hand. Bridge looked at her strangely.

"What'd you do, go shopping?!"

"Well there was nothing else for me to do."

"How 'bout working on the case?"

"You haven't given me anything else yet."

"You could always go back over what we had and see if you missed something or something else jumped out at you."

"It didn't," Nicole said.

"We're not here on a shopping trip you know."

"Did you really think I was just gonna sit here in this room the entire time you're gone?"

"Would've been nice to know we were both here with the same thing in mind."

"We are. I just wanted to see a little of the town before we really dug in. It's not like you were gonna take me anywhere or let me loose on my own. So I just did it myself."

"Do you have it out of your system now?"

"I dunno," Nicole said with a smile. "We'll see."

Bridge rolled his eyes and sighed. "And why didn't you answer your phone? I called you like three times to see where you were."

"Yeah, I saw. I just didn't feel like talking to you."

"Oh really?"

"I knew you'd ask where I was, then I'd tell you, then you'd start yelling at me like you're doing now. I just didn't want to listen to it."

"I'm not yelling."

"Well you're not talking nicely either."

"I am just making sure we're both here for the same

reason. We are getting paid to do a job, not buy out the stores on the street."

Nicole put her bags into her room. "Yeah, yeah, I got it. How'd your trip go? Find out anything at the airfield?"

"A little bit."

"That's it? That's all you're gonna tell me?"

"Oh, are you invested in our work now?"

Nicole put her hands on her hips and glared at him. "Are we done now? Can we move on?"

"I suppose so."

"Good. Now did you find out anything or not?"

"A little bit."

Nicole sighed out of frustration. "There are a couple of sharp things in those bags, so don't make me hit you over the head with it. Do you have something or not?"

Bridge smiled. "Just that the people at the airfield the helicopter tour guide worked isn't sure the thing went down."

"What do they think happened?"

"Apparently, the pilot was in some heavy debt to some unscrupulous characters due to some unpaid loans."

"So they think he was killed? What?"

"Or he tried to vanish somewhere, start anew someplace else."

"Could he do that?"

"The question isn't whether he could, it's whether he could be successful."

"How's that fit with Hower?"

"I'm not sure yet," Bridge answered. "I went up in a different chopper and went over the same exact route that Hower went on his tour."

"How do you know?"

"I asked."

"Oh."

"I looked all around while I was up there. There's no sign of debris anywhere on the ground, so if it crashed, someone did one hell of a clean up job."

"I still don't see how that fits with either Hower or Rodriguez."

"Hower I'm not sure. But if the pilot was into something, Rodriquez could've been one of the people he was in debt with. Or he was a middleman."

"You don't suppose Hower was actually one of the loans, do you?"

"What do you mean?"

"Well what if Hower is one of the supposed bad guys who loaned money to the pilot, either along with Rodriguez, or Rodriguez was working for Hower in collecting it?"

Bridge started nodding along, thinking of how it made sense. "So we're thinking of Hower as a victim and he could be a perpetrator."

"Well, in theory," Nicole replied. "Doesn't mean it's true. And even if it is, it doesn't mean he couldn't still be a victim.

"But that could explain the payments that Hower made to Rodriguez."

"He'd kind of be an expensive bill collector, though, wouldn't he? I mean, fifteen thousand dollars in total just for doing a job?"

"Well, five thousand a month… might not be that much. Especially if he's got loans out to more than one person."

"It would make sense."

"A lot of things might make sense," Bridge said. "It's just a matter of proving it."

"I have a feeling Mr. Hower might have been keeping some things from his wife."

"He wouldn't be the first."

"How do we go about proving it if it's true?"

"I think the key might be Mr. Rodriguez."

"If we can find him. And if he'll talk."

"That's the issue… finding him. The talking part… he'll talk. Once I find him, he'll talk."

"Confident in that are you?"

Bridge nodded. "Oh, he'll talk. It's just a matter of finding him first."

10

FOR THE NEXT THREE DAYS, Bridge looked for Rodriguez, or anyone who knew him. All he came up with, though, was dead ends. Nobody claimed to know him, and those that Bridge thought might, wouldn't admit to it. But it was still OK in Bridge's mind because he knew all the questions would somehow make it back to Rodriquez. It would have to make Rodriguez curious about who was asking around about him. Either it would make Rodriguez come out of hiding or it would send him scurrying to another part of the country for a few months until he was sure the pressure had been turned off. But Bridge was banking on the former. He kept asking about Rodriguez in a positive light, making it seem like he wanted to use his services, instead of making it seem like he wanted him in connection to something else. That was usually a surefire way of having someone hit the high road.

Bridge was at the hotel the Hower's usually stayed at, the one that Mrs. Hower saw her husband talking to Rodriguez in front of the building. He'd been there for a couple of hours, staking it out, seeing if Rodriguez would make an appearance. He had a picture of Rodriguez in his pocket for reference, so Bridge would be able to tell if his target showed up. As he sat at a table in the hotel bar area having a few drinks while he waited, his phone rang, his trusty partner wondering how he was making out.

"How's it going?" Nicole asked.

"Oh, you know, just great. Having a grand old time."

"What are you doing?"

"Just sitting here at the hotel bar, having a fruity drink, enjoying myself. You?"

"Just sitting here at my computer in my hotel room, not really having a grand old time."

"You sound depressed."

"I'm tired of sitting in here. For the last three days I've chained myself to this computer while you have all the fun out there."

"I wouldn't really call this fun," Bridge said.

"Nevertheless, it's gotta be better than what I'm doing. I'm sitting here staring out a window with nothing to do."

"So what do you wanna do?"

"I wanna get out there and help find this guy. I'm just gonna put it another way. If you don't let me out of this room I'm just gonna quit. Not that I really need your permission to do what I want, but I'm just saying."

Bridge knew she meant business. Whenever she mentioned she was going to quit, he knew she was near the breaking point. That was always her keyword to suggest she was just about done. He often just let her rant without interrupting, knowing it usually helped to calm her down.

"You say you don't like it here, but you want me chained to this computer twenty-four hours a day and I don't even have a lot to do on it."

"You're totally right," Bridge said.

Nicole wasn't even listening to him though, just continuing with her diatribe. "Wouldn't it make more sense for both of us to be out there? Wouldn't it be faster?"

"Absolutely."

"But no, you wanna do everything yourself, and I'm not even sure why."

"It's inexcusable on my part."

"Maybe because it's about what happened to you before down here, and you're afraid something might happen to me or something, but really, I'm a big girl. I can handle myself out there."

"I know you can."

"And for the life of me I just can't figure out what you're planning."

Bridge smiled and laughed to himself, wondering how long it was going to take her until she figured out

The Extractor

he was agreeing with everything she was saying. She obviously hadn't heard a word he was saying, probably blocking him out, assuming he was trying to talk her out of it. Finally, after a few minutes of her going off, she seemed to settle down.

"So do you have anything to say at all?" Bridge laughed again. "I don't see why you're laughing. What's so funny? You find this amusing?"

"No, I'm finding... well, yeah, I am finding it amusing actually."

"What do you find funny about this?"

"What I find funny is that I agree with every word you said."

"Well don't think that you're gonna... wait, what?"

"I agree with everything you've said."

"You do? What number drink are you on?"

"For the record, this is still my first. And if you had been paying any attention to me at all, you would have heard I agreed with you from the very first thing you said."

"Oh. You did?"

"Yes. You could have saved your voice from the thirty minutes of ranting you just did."

"It was not thirty minutes."

"Sure felt like it," Bridge said.

"Now who's dramatizing? So you're gonna let me help and not just sit here like a statue?"

Bridge took a deep breath before answering. "Yeah."

"You don't sound very enthusiastic."

"It's just… it's not that you're not capable. You obviously are. I count on you for everything and trust you completely. It's just… I guess when I'm here, I can't help but think about the partner I lost the last time I was here. I don't wanna lose you too."

"Awe, that almost sounded like a message of love."

"Really?"

"Listen, I understand you're hesitant about being here, I totally get that. But this is a totally different situation."

"It is but it's not."

"I'm not saying you have to let go of what happened before, but it's not the same situation. First off, I'm not trusting anyone else down here other than you, so you don't have to worry about me turning my back on anyone."

"Yeah, I guess."

"I'm not an amateur you know."

"I'm well aware of that," Bridge said.

"So don't treat me like one. I went to the same training academy you did. We both worked at the same agency. You might have a few years of field experience on me, but I'm not some rookie. We've been doing this for five years now."

"Has it been that long?"

"Yeah, it has. And when you asked me to join, we both knew we'd be getting into some tough situations, some dangerous ones. And we were both OK with that. We know the risks. Both of us. Not just you."

"You sure know how to beat a guy down, don't you? Jeez Louise, are you making me feel bad."

"Good. Sometimes you need that, you know."

"Yeah, I suppose."

"So now that I've uncuffed myself from the computer, what do you want me to do?"

"Might as well come down here and help me polish off a few drinks and wait for Rodriguez to show up."

"What makes you think he will?"

"Nothing. That's why I want you to come. That way if he doesn't show up I'm not drinking alone for the rest of the day."

"You sure know how to make a girl feel needed."

"It's a talent."

"I'm sure. OK, I'll be there in a jiffy."

"No hurry. Take your time."

Nicole quickly got ready to leave, making sure she had her gun on her, just in case. Though she didn't have the same fears about Mexico as her partner did, she still knew she had to be aware of what could happen. It was about twenty-five minutes from their hotel to the one Bridge was drinking at. While he was waiting for Nicole to arrive, he continued drinking, sipping slowly, and keeping his eyes peeled.

It wasn't even five minutes after getting off the phone that things started getting more interesting. A younger looking man, probably in his early twenties, came up to the bar and started conversing with the bartender. After a brief conversation that lasted only a few seconds, the bartender pointed over to Bridge's table. Bridge noticed, though he tried to be coy about it and pretend like it was no big deal. In truth, he knew one of two things was about to happen. Either someone was about to tell him he knew something about Rodriguez or someone was about to tell him to get lost. It had to be one of the two.

Bridge continued sitting calmly at the table, sipping his drink like nothing was going on. The man then walked over to his table and stood right in front of him, making sure he knew he was there. Bridge looked up at him with a curious expression.

"Something I can do for you?" The man pulled a chair out and sat down across from him. "Sure, sit down. I'd offer you a drink but I don't really know you that well."

"I hear you're looking for Ricardo Rodriguez."

"Who?"

"Don't be cute, man. Are you looking for him or not?"

"I'm looking for a lot of people," Bridge answered.

"So you some type of cop or something? Bounty hunter? What?"

"What I am is my business. Who are you?"

The man smiled. "That's my business."

"Cute. Is there something you want here?"

"Yeah, man, trying to find out what you want Rodriguez for?"

"What are you, friend of his? Or are you just the neighborhood snitch?"

The smile quickly faded from the man's face. "Yo, man, I ain't no snitch. And if you say something like that again you're gonna have a big problem on your hands."

"From who? You? Please. You're interrupting my drinking time here so if you've got nothing important to say to me, the door's over that way."

Though still not looking pleased, the man still stayed put in his chair. "If you want to find out anything about Rodriguez, you need to tell me what you want him for."

By the way the conversation was going, Bridge could tell the man was probably sent by Rodriguez himself, probably as a way of feeling out who he was or what he wanted. He definitely wasn't a snitch or informant. If he was, he would have already asked for money, or inquired as to whether there was some kind of payment available. In Bridge's experience, with all the informants he'd ever worked with, how much money was involved was usually one of the first three questions out of their mouths. They wouldn't have wasted time asking what they wanted a subject for. They didn't care as long as they got their money. No, this guy was feeling Bridge out. Bridge had to make sure he played it right. If he did, Rodriguez wouldn't be too far behind.

"What are you?" Bridge asked. "His lackey?"

"Yo, man, you're getting real close to having…"

"Yeah, yeah, I know, a problem, right? Why don't

you stop acting so tough and just tell me what you really want here? It's not like you're gonna intimidate me or something so just get on with it."

"You after him for something?"

Bridge just glared at him with one of those expressions that suggested he couldn't believe he really asked the question. "Really?"

"Are you really the best he could do?"

"What?"

"I mean, didn't he have anyone better that he could send to scout me out? 'Cause, I hope you don't mind me saying this, but you're terrible."

The man really didn't know how to respond now. Bridge was unlike anyone he had ever encountered before.

"Is there a price on Rodriguez' head?" the man asked.

"I wouldn't know. I'm not here for that."

"Then what are you here for? Yo, you might as well tell me, 'cause you ain't even gonna sniff him until you do. If you're after him, maybe I can help."

Bridge sighed, knowing the man wasn't going to go away until he answered. He played it off like he was really annoyed at having to answer the question.

"Fine, if you must know, about a month ago, I was talking to a guy named Bill Hower, who said he was doing business here with another guy named Ricardo Rodriguez. Hower said if I ever got down here, to look

The Extractor

Rodriguez up and see if we could work something out. That good enough for you?"

"Who's this Hower guy?"

"I dunno, some rich guy from up in the States. He said he'd given Rodriguez some money to do some jobs for him."

"And how do you know him?"

"Hower? I don't really. Well, he runs some consulting biz up there and he did some work for me. Got to talking and found out we had some mutual interests. Dig what I'm saying?"

"Maybe."

"So anyway, that's how I know him. We both have some of the same side interests, both like to visit Mexico, so here I am. Looking for someone I can do business with."

"And what kind of business are you looking to do?"

"I'm flexible. If there's money in it, I'm willing to get involved."

"It could get dangerous."

"Danger isn't a problem. Used to be in the military myself. Was in the Middle East doing a couple tours. I don't run the other way at the first sign of trouble."

"That's good. 'Cause if you wanna start doing business with Ricardo Rodriguez, trouble will find you."

"Bring it on."

The man smiled, slowly starting to appreciate Bridge's personality. "You done your drink?"

"I dunno. Why?"

"'Cause if you are, we're gonna take a little drive."

"To where?"

"You'll find out when you get there."

"Sounds mysterious," Bridge said. He then picked up his glass and chugged down the rest of his drink, putting it back on the table upside down. "Let's go."

11

The two men headed outside the bar when Bridge suddenly stopped.

"Is there a problem?"

"Well, yeah, actually there's a couple of them," Bridge replied.

"Like what?"

"Like first of all, I don't even know your name. And I have a personal policy of not going anywhere with anybody if I don't know who they are."

"So?"

"So I would like to know who I'm traveling with."

"I told you that's my business."

Bridge then turned around and headed back for the door to the hotel bar. "That's cool, bro, I don't need any of this. I can just take my business elsewhere for all I care. I don't need Rodriguez for anything. If you don't wanna tell me your name, fine. It's no problem. I'll just wait for one of the other people I put feelers out to to come find me."

"You put feelers out to others?"

Bridge smiled. "Sure did. You don't think you're the only game in town do you?"

The man looked around, then itched his forehead as he walked back to Bridge. "All right, man, all right. My name's Diego."

"Diego? Like Carmen San Dieg...," Bridge looked at the man's face and could tell he wasn't amused, not that he really cared whether he was or not. "No, I guess not."

"OK now? You know my name. We ready to go now?"

"Yeah, I guess so."

Bridge and Diego started walking, then Bridge stopped again. Diego caught Bridge stopping out of the corner of his eye and looked back at him.

"What now?"

"I got another small problem," Bridge answered.

Diego threw his arms up, obviously frustrated. "What is it this time?"

Bridge waited until Diego got closer to him, then started speaking in a soft tone, almost like he was afraid of anyone listening. "You see, it's like this... my girlfriend was on her way over here. She was supposed to meet me in about another ten minutes or so."

Diego looked at him, somewhat irritated by the stalling, not seeing a problem. "So?"

"Well then you showed up and we got this deal going on, but if I duck out on her, wowww, let me tell you, she will blow her top if I'm not here when she gets here."

"So?" Diego said with a shrug. "Get a new woman. There's plenty of them out there."

"Easier said than done my friend," Bridge said, laughing it up, slapping Diego on the shoulder. "To tell you the truth, she is great in bed, I mean, great in bed. I mean, she will do anything and I mean... *anything*. I mean, women like that just don't come along every day, am I right? Am I right? Come on, you know what I mean."

"I don't really care about your women issues, dude."

"Fair enough, fair enough, just give me ten more minutes, that's all I ask. Please. Then if she's not here by then, we can pick up and go. I'll buy you a drink at the bar as a special thank you, huh?"

Diego looked at the time, thinking it wouldn't hurt that much to wait a few more minutes. They had extra time. "Two drinks."

"You drive a hard bargain, my friend, a hard bargain. But two drinks it is." Bridge put his arm around the man's shoulder as they walked back into the bar. "I'll tell you what, if you play your cards right with this deal with Rodriguez, I might even hook you up with a few of my lady's friends, and let me tell you, a few of them are even wilder than she is. A few of them even like to do threesomes if that's your thing."

"Really?" Diego said with a smile, obviously liking the proposition more by the second.

"Oh yeah. I tried it before, but it really didn't do a whole lot for me personally, but if you're into it, I can make it happen for you."

"Really? What do they look like?"

"She has so many friends that... phew, let me tell you, they will all blow your mind." Bridge then laughed. "Ha, I didn't even mean to make that pun. But seriously, they got legs that will go on for miles, faces that could win beauty contests, and bosoms that could knock your eyes out."

Bridge and Diego sat down at a table and ordered their drinks as they waited for Nicole to arrive. Knowing that she was already on her way, Bridge wasn't too eager to go anywhere by himself without some backup. Especially if he was meeting Rodriguez. And he couldn't even be sure of that. Diego could have been some clown who was just trying to capitalize on Bridge somehow, maybe by robbing him, or had some other illegal act in mind.

But once Nicole got there, Bridge was going to have to play it off that they were a couple. There was no time to give Nicole advance notice as to what was going on, so he was going to have to take the lead and hope that she understood what was going on and followed along. He was pretty confident that she would since it wasn't the first time they'd been in a situation like that. Improvisation was something that sometimes went along with the job. They both knew it.

After ten minutes, Diego had finished both his drinks. He looked at the time and was ready to get going again.

"Looks like your lady friend ain't here. Maybe she ditched you."

"No, no, she would never do that," Bridge said. "Let's just give her five more minutes."

"Hey, the deal was ten."

"Five more minutes. Are you really willing to skip out on the time of your life with a couple seductive ladies just for five measly minutes?"

Diego thought about it, then nodded. "One more drink?"

Bridge smiled. "You're a hard man to do business with. One more drink it is."

Bridge ordered another drink, but looked over at the door, hoping Nicole would get there soon. He looked at the time and figured it was right around when she should have been getting there. He hoped she got there soon since he wasn't sure how much longer he could keep Diego busy. If all else failed, he supposed he could keep buying him drinks, but it wasn't his intention to get the man drunk. Then he wouldn't have led him to where Rodriguez was.

Bridge tried to get Diego to drink slower this time, but it didn't do much good. The man seemed like drinking was a hobby to him as he gulped his drink down as fast as he did the others. The man then turned his glass over, signifying he was done.

"OK, no more amigo, time to go."

"One more?" Bridge asked.

"No, no, no more. If I show up for a meeting with Ricky and I'm drunk he'll shoot me."

"Oh, we can't have that then, can we?"

"Come on, let's go."

Bridge took one last look at the door and sighed, realizing he was going into this thing without backup. But, it was one of the perils of the job. Sometimes it just had to go down like that. Bridge then finished his own drink, then stood up. As he did, he looked over at the door and saw Nicole strutting in. Bridge got a huge smile on his face, thankful she finally showed up. He put his arms out as she approached.

"Nicky, my love."

Nicole instantly recognized the clue, as he only ever called her Nicky when there was something wrong or the situation was unusual. In normal times, he always called her Nicole or Nic. She saw the young, thin man standing next to Bridge and figured something was up. She played along, not that it was much trouble, since it involved being affectionate. Getting cuddly with him was always one of the perks of the job and didn't require much of a strain on her part. She sauntered right up to him and put her arms around him as they embraced. They then passionately kissed each other on the lips, then hugged again.

"I'm sorry I'm late, dear, but you know how I am with my shoes. I passed by a store on the way here and I just couldn't resist taking a peek inside."

"Oh, that's OK," Bridge said. "I was just sitting here with my new friend Diego having a few drinks."

"Oh really?"

"Yeah, I was just telling him about some of your friends, how they like to get a little kinky sometimes. He's kind of into that sort of thing."

"Oh, yeah, I was just talking to a couple of them last night. They were asking me if I knew anyone for them." Nicole then gave Diego a lustful eye. "You look like exactly the type of guy they'd go for."

Diego couldn't help but show a wide smile. "Oh really?"

"Oh yeah. You'll have to give me your phone number for them. I'll give it right to them."

Diego went over to the bar and grabbed a napkin and a pen and instantly wrote down his number to hand over to the pretty lady. Nicole took the napkin and put it in her purse.

"I hope you really are interested because they hate it when men just play games with them and stand them up or something."

"Whenever they're ready," Diego said.

Bridge looked at Nicole with a certain kind of glance, shaking his head, not believing how easy it was with some men. Just mention a few pretty girls and sex and some men just lose their minds. They forget which head they're thinking with.

"It might be a few days," Nicole said. "But you'll be contacted I'm sure."

"Can't wait," Diego replied. He then turned his attention back to Bridge. "You ready now?"

"Ready?" Nicole asked. "Where are we going? I thought we were going to eat lunch here then go shopping."

"Ugh, I'm so sorry, sweetie," Bridge said. "I met Diego and we're gonna talk a little business first. As soon as I get back I'll make it up to you."

"You better. I've got a fresh new pair of handcuffs back at the hotel waiting for some usage." Nicole gave him a devilish type of smile, enjoying talking like that to him.

Bridge could tell she was enjoying herself. He smiled at her, knowing she really meant every word she was saying. It wasn't hard for her to make something up. Bridge looked over at Diego, who was smiling at him, who wouldn't have minded such an activity himself.

Nicole started seductively playing with Bridge's shirt collar. "Why do men have to talk business all the time? Especially at the expense of other such fun activities."

"Well, it won't be too long, right Diego? Be back in no time?"

"Assuming all goes well."

The Extractor

"I think I might need another pair of shoes out of this deal as well," Nicole said.

Bridge then kissed her on the cheek. "Whatever you want, darling."

Nicole then wrapped her arms around Bridge's neck, playing it up for all it was worth. "Fine. I guess I can let you go for a few hours. One more kiss before you go?"

Bridge grinned, realizing what she was doing. "OK, but only one more. Have to talk business, you know?"

"If you must."

They then engaged in another passionate kiss, Nicole really enjoying it. Not that Bridge didn't too, but he really was trying to keep somewhat of a wall between them so they didn't cross that line. It was hard sometimes though. He really did find her very attractive, and role playing like this didn't help to keep him from crossing that line. Sometimes in moments like this, he wanted to just say the hell with it and get into that relationship with her that she desperately wanted. But he always managed to keep it professional, no matter how hard it was.

"Don't be too long now," Nicole said, finally taking her arms off him.

"Well, if I was, I'm sure you would *follow* me, right?" Bridge made sure he put some extra emphasis on the word, making sure she understood to follow them.

Nicole easily picked up on the cue though. "Oh, I definitely would. All over."

12

It was a long car ride to meet with Rodriguez. Bridge got into Diego's car, who also did the driving. They'd been on the road for roughly thirty minutes and there didn't seem to be an end in sight. And they weren't even going around in circles. Bridge paid careful attention to road signs and landmarks, just to make sure they weren't doing just that. It wouldn't have been the first time someone tried to fool him by trying to pass off it was a longer drive, just by driving in a circle when the real destination was only ten minutes away. This wasn't that though. Bridge periodically looked in the side mirror to make sure Nicole was following. He made sure he didn't keep turning around as that would have been a dead giveaway that someone was tailing them. He needed to make sure that Nicole was a surprise. He did notice their rental car keeping a safe distance behind them.

The Extractor

"How much longer is it?" Bridge asked, getting a tad impatient.

"Few more minutes."

"Few more as in two or three or a few more as in ten or twenty?"

Diego smiled. "A few more."

Bridge rolled his eyes then looked back out the window. The few more minutes actually turned into another twenty. The car finally came to a stop just outside what looked like a small place of business. Diego got out of the car and stood near the hood. Bridge slowly got out as well, looking the building over to figure out what it was. It was well outside the city and sitting all by itself on a sideroad without much else near it. Bridge didn't really like the location as it would've been a prime place for someone to be setting him up. There was no one around to hear any screams. But he also knew places like this was usually where people like Rodriguez operated out of.

"So what's this?" Bridge asked, joining Diego near the hood. "Don't tell me this is where he lives?"

Diego laughed. "Don't be silly. You think Rodriguez would live in a dump like this?"

"Then what are we doing here?"

"Hey, Ricky says to bring you here, I bring you here."

"What's this, his meeting place?"

"Sometimes."

"Is he here? I don't see any other cars."

"He parks in the back. He don't like to advertise where he's at if he can help it."

"Smart. Very smart."

"Yeah. So let's go. You're the one who wanted this, remember? Unless you wanna walk back to town."

"Walk? What, I don't get a ride?"

Diego smiled. "Not unless Rodriguez says so."

"Oh. I hope everything goes well then."

The two men then approached the front door of the two thousand square foot building. As Diego opened the door, Bridge took a quick peek behind to see if he noticed Nicole anywhere nearby. He didn't see her. Hopefully things didn't take a quick turn for the worse once he stepped inside, because if it did, help might be a little long in coming.

Diego stepped inside, closely followed by Bridge. Before he could even close the door, Bridge felt a sharp pain on the top of his head, something heavy crashing down on it. He immediately fell to the floor and held the top of his head. He took his hand off his head and held it in front of his face to check for blood, though there were no signs of it. He sure had a massive headache though. He was on all fours, though not for long as he suddenly was lifted into the air like he was flying. Two burly men had picked him up, one on each side of him, Bridge's feet off the ground. Bridge looked at the two of them, both of whom were bald with facial hair. One had a goatee, and one had a beard. They were both fierce looking though.

"Hey guys, how's it going?" Bridge asked with a laugh, hoping to diffuse any tension. Neither of the men responded to him though. Bridge looked around and saw Diego standing nearby. "Hey, buddy, what's going on here?"

Diego shrugged. "Search me. I was just told to bring you here."

"Umm, if there's a problem, I can just go back, walking is not a problem."

"Well let's just wait for Ricky and see what he has to say."

"You know what, I don't even need to see him anymore. It's no problem, really. I can talk to him another time if that's better."

"We'll just wait."

After a few more seconds, the burly men carried Bridge into another room, one which was barely lit. It was so poorly lit that Bridge associated the room with being in a dungeon somewhere. The men plopped Bridge onto a shaky wooden chair and then tied him to it. The chair was so unstable that Bridge thought he was going to collapse on it. He shook it a few times, but still stayed upright. The two men that carried Bridge in then left, leaving him to himself, as far as he could tell. He tried looking around the room, though he could barely see a few inches in front of him.

"Hey guys?! Diego?! Anybody?! It's perfectly OK, if you want me to go away, just say so, I'll walk back to town and you'll never see me again. You have my word."

Bridge struggled to see into the darkness, thinking that he saw some sort of mass move through it, though he couldn't be sure. He got the feeling that he wasn't alone though. It felt like he was being watched. Whether it was someone close or far, he couldn't be sure, but he could almost feel the eyes staring at him.

If this was the first time he'd been thrown into a deep dark hole he might have started to get nervous or beginning to panic. Luckily from some of his previous adventures, both during his time in the CIA and since then, he'd been in similar situations several times. So he kind of knew what to expect, though a person could never be exactly sure what was going to be around when the lights came back on. From his experience, though, it was usually one of two things. Rodriguez would come out of the woodwork and start talking to him, trying to figure out what he wanted, or, someone would start beating the tar out of him. Bridge obviously hoped for Rodriguez to show up. He really didn't want to be on the receiving end of the punches from the two guys that lifted him up when he went through the door. They looked like they threw with mean intentions. Plus, the last time he was in a situation like this, he almost broke a rib.

Bridge wasn't sure how long his stint in the darkness would last. It could have been only for a few minutes, or it might wind up lasting a few hours. It usually depended on the mood of his captors and what they were looking for. He also thought about Nicole. Though he was reasonably sure she was out there, somewhere, hopefully not too far away, he also wasn't completely sure she didn't take a wrong turn somewhere along the way. He didn't see her car for the last few minutes before they arrived, and he didn't see her just before he went inside, so he was taking it on blind faith that she found her way there. Of course, maybe he wouldn't need her to rescue him, but if things got dicey, and she wasn't there, it would get a whole lot more dicey.

After sitting there silently for close to thirty minutes, Bridge moved his head slightly to the left. He thought he heard a footstep, though it equally could have been his imagination. Then it sounded like a door closed, though ever so faintly, like someone was trying their best to not make a sound. He had a feeling that whatever was going to happen, was about to happen soon. He wasn't wrong. Only a few minutes later, Bridge felt a hand touch his shoulder, causing his body to flinch. All the lights in the room suddenly turned on, though it didn't do a whole lot for the ambience of the place. Even with all the lights on, it still was pretty dimly lit, though at least Bridge could now see the walls of the room.

Bridge turned his head and could tell that there was someone behind him, which always made him a little nervous when he couldn't tell what that person was doing. Whoever was behind him could have had an ax, waiting to chop his head off for all he knew. Even though he knew that was probably unlikely, it still ran through his mind. There wasn't anybody else in the room though. With someone standing behind him, Bridge figured that was about to change, unless the man was just standing there for his health, which he probably wasn't.

"Hey, uhh, I can't see your face back there, but would you mind untying me here? It's starting to chafe my arms a little." After waiting a few seconds, and not getting a response, Bridge figured the man wasn't the talkative type. "I guess that's a no, huh? That's all right, I just figured I'd ask. Could you, uhh, could you tell me how long I'm gonna sit here for? Not that I really mind, just wondering."

The man behind him still didn't respond, not that Bridge really expected him to. He was just hoping to move things along. He was getting tired of sitting there, letting his mind wander. Even if he was about to get whipped, he'd rather just get it over with then wondering if he was about to get pulverized. At least then he'd know where he stood with these people. And he'd know who they were. Right now, he still didn't know much of anything. Diego said he was with Rodriguez, but he could have just been saying that to lure him there. He could have been with anybody.

"Hey, bud, what do I do if I have to go potty or something?" Bridge looked down at the dirty, dusty, old wooden floors that looked like they hadn't been cleaned in quite some time. "I'd hate to get these floors wet, you know, they look like they just got a good wax and shine."

A door then opened, a man walking in, with Diego right behind him. Bridge didn't need an introduction to recognize the face. It was Rodriguez. He looked the same as he did in the pictures that Bridge had seen of him. Rodriguez had a cocky looking grin on his face, seemingly taking pleasure in Bridge's situation. He walked around the room for a bit, sizing Bridge up. For his part, Bridge also wore a grin on his face, not wanting to make it seem like he was nervous or anything.

"Diego, buddy, how's it going, man?" Diego didn't respond either. "You know, I'm starting to feel a little hostility in here. I'm tied up, I talk to people, no one talks back, it's almost like people don't like me or something. I mean, what's going on here?"

Rodriguez finally stopped pacing around the room, standing directly in front of Bridge, looking down at him. "You really do ramble on a lot about nothing, don't you?"

"Well, you know how it is, some of us are just blessed with those sweet and sexy voices, so we just feel we have to show it off sometimes."

Rodriguez laughed. "You're a funny man too, eh?"

"What are you, Canadian?"

"You know who I am?"

"Yeah, you're Ricky Ricardo… I mean, Rodriguez. Sorry, I always get those names mixed up."

Rodriguez smiled, not taking offense to it. He actually thought the man was kind of amusing. "You have me at a disadvantage in that you seem to know me, but the same cannot be said the other way around."

"The name's Luke."

"I'm sure you have a last name."

"Bridgerton."

"So you're the man that's been asking a lot of questions about me over the past few days."

"Yeah, and I have to say, I don't really appreciate being left tied up in a chair in a dark room for, what, must be close to forty minutes now?"

"I'm sure you must realize precautions must be taken when we do business with people we don't know."

"Well, now you know me."

"What is it that you want Mr. Bridgerton?"

"Same thing everybody wants. To make money."

"And I assume your plans involve me in some capacity?"

"Could be. If you want to make more money that is."

"It would depend on the idea… and the amount of money that we're talking about."

"The plan involves drug smuggling and counterfeiting. The money could be in excess of well over five million a month."

Rodriguez raised his eyebrows. His facial expression indicated he was interested in something that would bring in that amount of money. Of course, he needed to hear more about the plan first. "That's a lot of money."

"And that's just the beginning. We could be talking about something that brings in hundreds of millions of revenue every year."

"What makes you think I can help?"

"Please. Everyone knows you're a facilitator. You can make things happen."

Rodriguez tilted his face, pleased to hear the compliment, agreeing with the sentiments. "I do have some talents in that regard."

"I talked to Bill Hower some time ago, and he told me he was using you for some stuff, so I figured I would do the same."

"Bill Hower?"

"Yeah, he told me he was paying you a few thousand dollars for something, we didn't get into details, but he spoke highly of you."

"The name doesn't ring a bell."

"Really? Because he was down here just a few weeks ago. As a matter of fact, some people say he was killed in a helicopter crash along with some pilot who was into some other stuff. Now me personally, I'm not sure he's dead, well, neither of them really, or who was the intended target, but that's a discussion for another day."

"Hower?" Rodriguez said, trying to make it seem like he was really thinking about it. "Oh yeah, I remember now. I just did a few small jobs for him, nothing big. Certainly nothing in the realm of the numbers that you're talking about."

"That's because Bill always aimed low. I always have my sights set for the sky. What was he doing, some minor drug deals or something?"

"That's… not relevant to our discussion."

"Oh, OK, fair enough." Bridge started wiggling around in his chair, trying to free himself of the ropes that bound him there. "You think we could do something about these? They're really starting to irritate me."

"I think we're fine as we are."

"If we're gonna do business together, we're gonna have to trust and respect each other, right? Letting me out of this would be a good start."

"Yeah, well, maybe. I haven't decided yet if we're gonna do business. I need to do some checking on you first. Make sure you're on the level."

"What? Really? And how long's that gonna take?"

"As long as it takes to find out who you really are."

"I already told you."

"Then it won't take long at all. But if you're lying about all this, and I find out your name isn't really Luke Bridgerton, then you're gonna wish you never came here."

"Everything I told you is completely one hundred percent accurate."

"We'll see. If it's not, you won't ever be getting up out of that chair. Alive that is."

13

ONCE RODRIGUEZ and his cohorts left the room, they once again turned off the lights, leaving Bridge in complete darkness once more.

"Not this again."

Bridge sighed, knowing he was in a lot of trouble. As soon as they started checking on him they would discover Bridgerton wasn't his real name. That was the name he checked in with at the hotel, and the name he kept flashing around when he was asking questions, but he was sure Rodriguez would go a lot deeper than that. He would most likely check all his contacts, and even people in the government to get in deeper on Bridge's background. Once they discovered that Bridge wasn't actually known to anybody in the drug world, Rodriguez would have plenty of doubts about his story. And he probably wouldn't trust him either. Even if Bridge told him he was a newbie in the drug world, it was unlikely that Rodriguez would put any faith into him at all.

There wasn't much question in Bridge's mind what would happen when Rodriguez returned. He'd most likely get beaten up for a while, probably breaking a few bones in the process, trying to draw out of him who he really was and what he was doing there. If he was lucky, they'd leave it at that. If his luck had run out, they wouldn't stop at the beating and would put a bullet in his head. The only real question in Bridge's mind was how long it would take for them to get back.

Bridge sat there for a few more minutes, trying to wriggle free from his constraints, though he had no luck in doing so. It didn't feel like he made any progress at all. After another ten minutes evaporated, Bridge picked his ears up, thinking he heard something coming from just outside the door. It sounded kind of like a thud, but he couldn't be sure. He assumed his visitors had returned.

"That was a quick check," he said to himself.

Knowing he wasn't breaking himself free, Bridge started to ready himself for the beating that he was sure to commence soon. They were going to find out Bridgerton wasn't his real name and whatever hopes he had of getting in with Rodriguez were flushed down the toilet. The door opened up, and since it was dark, Bridge couldn't see who it was, but he sighed and braced himself for whatever was coming his way. But he wasn't quite ready for what was actually there. He felt a hand touch his left shoulder, and Bridge's body tensed up slightly, a shiver going through him. Then he felt another hand, this time on his right shoulder. The hands started massaging his shoulders, and Bridge could tell they were the hands of a woman. Then Bridge felt the hands on his head, tilting his head to the side, feeling a pair of luscious lips kiss the side of his neck.

"Is this the foreplay before the beatdown?" Bridge asked.

"No beatdown involved," the woman replied. "Unless you like it that way."

Bridge might not have minded if this part continued, as long as it wasn't followed by the second part. "No, no, we can skip that."

The woman then moved around to the front of him, all while keeping her hands on him. She stood in front of him, giving Bridge a real good glimpse of her.

"Nicole!" Bridge yelled, though it was more like a loud whisper. "What are you doing here?"

"Didn't you want me to follow you?"

"Yes. I mean, what are you doing in here?"

"I came to rescue you. You looked like you needed some help."

"Gee, thanks. You think you could've done it without all the hanky panky?"

Nicole smiled. "You didn't really think I could let an opportunity like this pass, did you?"

"Very funny, just untie me before they get back."

Nicole rubbed her chin, thinking about the proposition. "I don't know. You are in an extremely favorable position for me since you can't get away or fight back."

"Really? You're really gonna do this now? They might be back any minute."

"No, we're good. There was only one of them outside the door and I took care of him. The rest of them left a while ago. I figure we still have plenty of time."

"Doing something against someone's will is still against the law you know."

"Is it really against your will?"

Bridge thought for a few seconds. "Well… that's a question for another time. I'm not exactly comfortable just hanging out here."

"I wish you were just hanging out here."

"Nicole! Can we please just go?!"

Nicole then rubbed his knee just to tease him. "Oh, fine. You're such a stick-in-the-mud."

"Really? Just untie me please."

Nicole started to reach for the ropes, but then pulled her arms back. "I dunno."

"What?! What do you mean, I don't know. Just untie me."

"Well, I got you in such a favorable position, maybe I should use it to my advantage."

"I told you, not now."

"I don't mean that. At least not here. I mean, maybe I should get you to agree to my terms first."

"Terms? You have terms?!"

"Well, let's just call it suggestions."

"Such as what?!"

"Oh, I dunno, maybe like you actually take me to dinner on, like, a real date."

Bridge closed his eyes and sighed, knowing he was in no position to argue. "Fine. One date."

"Well, maybe a few. One sometimes isn't enough to know if you're really into a person, you know?"

Bridge took a deep breath. "Fine. Three dates."

"Well… I suppose that'll be good enough."

"Great. Now untie me."

"Fantastic," Nicole said. "Now for the other things."

"Other things?! You mean there's more?!"

"Oh yeah. That was just for starters."

"Starters? Really? Can we please just talk about this later? I promise I'll agree to anything you want. Just get me out of here?"

"But later you'll be in more of a position to say no."

"Also three massages," Nicole said.

"For who?"

"Me."

"You want me to give you massages?"

Nicole gave a devilish smile. "Yep. Anytime, anyplace, of my choosing. And any attire I choose."

Bridge looked up, even though he couldn't see anything up there. "Fine," he whined. "Whatever you want. Please just get me out of here."

"Then there's the other things…"

"Nicole!!"

"Yes?"

"I agree to everything! Everything you want. Whatever it is, I don't care, just get me out of here. If you want me to undress in front of you every night, shower in your presence for a month, kiss your feet, rub your shoulders, tickle your funny bone, I don't care, just get me out of here!"

"Wow, this worked out so much better than I had imagined it would upon coming in here."

"I'm sure it has, please just untie me."

Nicole reached over and finally got Bridge untied, cutting the ropes with her knife. Bridge then stood up and started rubbing his arms. Nicole started laughing about the situation.

"What's so funny?" Bridge asked.

"Just this. Who would've thought The Extractor needed extracting himself. I'm extracting The Extractor."

"Oh, that's a riot. That's just a ball of laughs."

Nicole grinned. "I thought so."

"Why don't you just keep it up for a while?"

"No, that's all right. We should be going."

"Oh, are we ready to go now?"

"I'm ready when you are. You're the one moving slow."

"Me?! Who's the one who wouldn't let me go unless a host of conditions were met?"

"Can you get off that now so we can just go?"

"Oh, so you're in a hurry now, are you?"

"Well, you wanna stay here all day or what?" Nicole asked.

"Oh, you're just on a roll today, aren't you?"

They finally stopped their bantering and rushed over to the door. They peeked out, making sure no one else was there, other than the man still lying on the floor that Nicole took care of on the way in. Bridge looked down at the man and saw he still wasn't moving.

"He dead?"

"No, just gave him one of my specials," Nicole answered.

"Which one is that?"

"Just walked up to him, shoved a needle in his arm, and off to sleep he went."

Bridge looked at her like she was crazy. "What are you doing, just walking around with jacked up needles full of bye-bye juice?"

Nicole looked at him like he was the crazy one for asking. She didn't see anything wrong with it. "Why not? You've got to be prepared at all times, right?"

"How many other things are you carrying around in that purse of yours?"

"Just the necessities."

Bridge's eyes widened, then shook the thoughts out of his head. He didn't even want to know what she considered necessities. For all he knew, she was carrying hand grenades and bazookas in there. Nicole then turned half-way around to show him the bag on her back.

"It's a backpack, not a purse. I don't carry purses on matters like this. It's not like I'm going to a formal dinner or something."

"I stand corrected."

"Where are we going after we leave here?" Nicole asked.

"I dunno. Back to your car I guess."

"I gathered that much. I meant after that."

"Oh. I guess back to the hotel so we can regroup. Getting a hold of Rodriguez to tell us about Hower's gonna be a little trickier now."

"A little?"

"OK, hard, difficult, nearly impossible, but not impossible."

"That didn't really make sense, you know. You said impossible twice."

"Just don't worry about it, OK? Stop critiquing my english language skills and focus on getting out of here."

"So what are you jabbering on for?" Nicole asked. "Stop talking and lead the way."

"Oh, well, I didn't actually see which way's the exit. You see, I had difficulty seeing when they brought me in here, so if you wanna do the honors…"

Nicole rolled her eyes and shook her head. "Fine, I'll lead the way."

They stepped through the door and over the lifeless

body of the knocked-out man. They took a few more steps through the darkened hallway when they heard a noise that sounded like a door slamming shut.

"Uhh, that didn't sound good," Bridge said.

"No it did not."

"I thought you said we were alone."

"We were. At least, we were when I came in."

They stood there, paralyzed by what they thought might have been nearby, not wanting to move into a bad situation, especially when they had a hard time seeing.

"I really think we should be going," Nicole said.

They started hearing a few more noises, sounding like a bunch of feet shuffling around on the dirty concrete floor.

"Uhh, Nicole, I have a feeling we're not alone anymore."

A voice then boomed through the hallway, sounding very familiar. "How right you are, Mr. Bridgerton. How right you are."

The lights in the hallway then started flickering, revealing Rodriguez toward the end of it, with about ten of his men standing right behind him.

"Umm, yeah, I think you're right," Nicole said. "We're definitely not alone anymore."

"So what are we gonna do?"

"I don't know. You're The Extractor. Figure out a way to extract us."

"Now is not the time for a play on words."

"Luke, just get us out of here."

"I'm thinking."

"Think faster."

"You can't rush greatness."

"You can't rush dead either," Nicole replied.

"Well we're not dead… not yet at least."

14

Rodriguez and his men started inching closer, causing Bridge and Nicole to falter backwards, stumbling over the knocked-out man.

"Wait, why don't we just go out the other door?" Bridge said.

"What other door?"

"I dunno, but there's gotta be one, right? Every place has a front and a back door. If they're blocking one, there's gotta be another."

"Lead the way."

Bridge and Nicole then turned around and started running down the hallway, opposite the direction that Rodriguez and his men were coming from. They only got a few feet before they were stopped in their tracks by the sight of an additional group of men marching toward them. They looked in both directions and knew this was not going to be pretty.

"I think we have a problem," Nicole said.

"You don't say?"

"What are we gonna do?"

"Well, looks to me like we got two choices."

"Which are?"

"Considering there are no other hallways to run into, and these ones are blocked, we can take our chances by running into one of these groups."

Nicole didn't seem to like that option. "And the other choice?"

"We can go back into that room and see if there's an exit somewhere."

"They're not just gonna put you in a room with a door or a window."

"I didn't say a door," Bridge said. "We might be able to get into the ceiling somehow, or maybe a ventilator shaft or something."

"I don't like either of those choices."

"Well I guess there's a third choice."

"Yeah? What's that?"

"We can just give ourselves up."

"I hate that choice too."

"Feel free to come up with your own."

Nicole started doing just that. Though she wasn't the one known as The Extractor, she was pretty crafty herself at getting out of sticky situations. Breathing heavily, she slowed down for a second as she thought of something that just might work. It would never be confused with one of their best escape plans, but it sure would be memorable if it worked.

"I got something," Nicole said, reaching into her pocket.

Bridge looked down at her hand as it came out of her pocket, holding something. "What the hell is that?"

Nicole grinned at him. "You'll see." She then held the rectangular object up in the air, high over her head. "All right," she yelled, loud enough for everyone to hear. "Let us out of here, or I'll throw this bomb down on the floor and kill all of us."

Rodriguez laughed, not taking the threat seriously. "You're joking. You wouldn't kill yourself."

"Well I'm sure not gonna let you do it for me. Just let us through or you'll be the first one to go."

"I don't believe you."

"Oh you don't, huh?"

"No, I don't. I think if you had a bomb you would have used it already."

"Don't test me Rodriguez."

"Yeah, don't test her," Bridge said. "She means business."

"I think you're bluffing," Rodriguez said.

"Oh I am, huh?" Nicole replied. "Well what do you think I'm holding then?"

Rodriguez looked at it carefully, and even from his distance, could see that it wasn't a bomb. "It looks like... a candy bar."

Bridge looked horrified at the thought and immediately turned his head, looking up at his partner's hand. It was a candy bar. He could see the writing on the wrapper.

"Seriously?" Bridge said. "That's the best you could do? A candy bar?!"

"I thought it might work."

"What were you planning to do, melt them to death?!"

"Well I didn't hear you coming up with any ideas."

"We gotta get in that room."

"No, there's probably nothing in there. I doubt they shoved you in a room where there was a method of escape."

"Nicole, we're running out of time! Stop fighting me."

Nicole then turned her back to him. "Just reach inside my pack and grab a couple of the smoke bombs."

"Smoke bombs?"

"Yeah, there's a couple in there."

"You've had smoke bombs in there this entire time and you didn't say anything?"

"I wanted to see if we could get out of this first."

"Really?! With what, a candy bar? What is this, some type of game?"

"Oh stop complaining and just do it." As Bridge reached into her bag, Nicole noticed the men starting to move closer to them. "Hurry up, we're running out of time."

"I got it, I got it." Bridge removed the smoke bombs and handed one of them to Nicole.

"Should we give them the chance to get out of the way first?"

"The hell with that."

Bridge immediately tossed his smoke bomb toward the men on his side, then Nicole tossed hers toward Rodriguez and his crew. The smoke immediately dispensed into the air and all the people started dispersing everywhere to avoid hacking their lungs up.

"This wasn't well thought out," Nicole said. "We still gotta get through them."

"Yeah, but we've been trained to deal with these types of things."

"Plus I got goggles back there so it doesn't get in our eyes."

Bridge just shook his head. He didn't know why he was surprised at how or why she brought the things she did. But she was always on top of everything. That was probably why she was so invaluable to him. She always thought of everything. They each put on a pair of goggles to avoid the smoke getting in their eyes. They then started running toward the exit, running past the men who were coughing. Bridge and Nicole held their breath in to avoid breathing in the smoke.

As they ran past a few of the men, some of them tried to stop them from getting around them. Bridge walloped a couple of the men across their faces, easily sending them to the floor. Nicole did the same, though she was a little more adept with her feet, thanks to her karate training. Once Bridge and Nicole finally found the end of the hallway, they pushed open the door leading outside to where Nicole came in at. But they still weren't free yet. A couple of the men inside beat them out there, getting out of the smoke filled corridor. They were still coughing, but noticed the intruders had joined them outside. Rodriguez and Diego were among them. Realizing they were about to have another battle, Bridge knew they were going to have a tough time in leaving.

"Nic, hurry and get the car!"

She hurried off immediately, realizing he was sending her away so she didn't have to deal with the onslaught that was coming. Though Rodriguez stayed back, not liking getting his hands dirty, his five cohorts lunged at Bridge, Diego being the first one to get to him. Bridge decked him with a right cross.

Bridge pointed to him as he stood over him. "That's for being a rotten friend."

The other four men then jumped on top of Bridge, each getting a few shots in. Bridge wrestled around with the men as they all hit the dirt. Diego got up and then joined the fray. After a minute, they all stood up, the five men each getting a turn at hitting Bridge. Bridge tried to return the favors, but wasn't able to do much damage against so many. The men then pushed him up against the wall and held his arms so he couldn't fire off any more punches.

With the situation now under control, and with seemingly no risk of being injured, Rodriguez then moved closer to the action. Diego stood just to the back of him. Only a few inches away from Bridge, Rodriguez sought answers.

"Who are you and why are you here?"

Before Bridge was able to say something sarcastic, they all heard an engine rumbling, revving up, sounding like it was getting closer to them. They turned around, only to see a light blue car racing towards them. They all jumped out of the way as, with Nicole in the driver seat, it didn't seem intent on stopping. As everyone scattered, Nicole slammed on the brakes, almost putting her foot through the floor. Bridge's eyes widened, feeling like he was about to get hit, though he didn't move. He just closed his eyes, waited, and braced for impact. He assumed he was going to feel a lot of pain. With the tires squealing, then suddenly stopping, Bridge opened his eyes, only to see the car stopped in front of him. He looked down at his knees and saw maybe an inch of space between him and the vehicle, if that. He then looked up at the sky as if to say thank you. Nicole then leaned out the window.

"Let's go! Get in!"

Bridge then ran around to the side of the car, taking the liberty of landing one more shot to the jaw of Diego, who was the only person who was still nearby. Once Bridge got in, Nicole floored it in reverse, almost running over three of them, who once again jumped out of the way. Nicole then pushed the pedal to the floor and sped out of there.

Bridge then leaned out the window and started shouting. "You're a lousy friend, Diego. You can forget about that three-way with her lady friends now, Bucko!"

Nicole looked at him and shook her head. "You say it like he's actually losing something. There was no three-way."

"Yeah, but he doesn't know that. Let the crumb think he's losing something."

Nicole looked in the mirror and saw a couple of cars start to follow them. "They're coming."

"Figured they would. You're gonna have to do some fancy driving here to get us out of this one."

"No problem."

"And what was with that trick you pulled back there?!"

"What trick?"

"You almost took my knees out."

"But I didn't."

"But you almost did," Bridge said. "If you had hesitated for one more second, I'd be in a wheelchair for the rest of my life."

"So? There are worse things than being in a wheelchair."

"Yes, I know, and one of those is being dead. And I could've been that too if you were any later."

"Oh, stop bellyaching. You're fine, everything's fine."

"Everything is not fine." Bridge then leaned out the window to look at their pursuers again. "They're gaining on us. Things are not fine."

Nicole pointed to the glove compartment. "There's some things in there that should slow them down."

Bridge glared at her out of the corner of his eye, not sure if he even wanted to look. Who knew what she had hidden in there? It could have been anything. He cautiously opened the glove compartment, turning his head, leaning back, and squinting, half-expecting it to blow up once he opened it. Once he saw it wasn't rigged with some type of explosive, which wouldn't have shocked him considering who was driving, he reached in and put his hands on a couple of grenades. He pulled them out and held them on his lap.

"Really, Nic? Grenades?"

Nicole shrugged, keeping an eye on their pursuers through the mirror. "What's the matter?"

"I mean, really? This is a rental! You've got a couple of grenades just hanging out in a rental car."

"Figured I'd carry them around in case we needed them. Now we need them."

"What if someone started shooting at us and the bullets penetrated the car and struck them?"

"Then I guess we'd blow up."

"That's not very reassuring."

"It wasn't meant to be."

"What's next, a bazooka in the trunk?" Nicole glanced over at him and smiled. Bridge just shook his head. "I shouldn't have asked. You do have something back there, don't you?"

"A girl has to be prepared at all times."

"Unbelievable. I'm not even gonna ask what's back there? It's probably… no, no, I'm not even gonna speculate. I'm just letting it be."

"Instead of jacking your jaws while you're just sitting there, why don't you toss those suckers at the people chasing us?"

"We are moving kinda fast."

"Well if you don't think you're good enough to get them, then just take the wheel and I can do it."

Bridge put his arm out to keep her in her seat. "Just keep your pants on. I didn't say I couldn't do it. I just have to calculate everything in my mind due to the speed we're going, that's all."

Nicole grinned. "What's the matter? Afraid of being shown up by me."

"I'm not afraid of being shown up."

"Oh? Well, I got you out of that room, then I was the one who brought the smoke bombs, then I was the one who got the car, then I was the one who saved you outside again, and I'm the one who's driving away. Feeling a little jealous?"

"Don't be ridiculous. It's not about who gets the credit for doing things. It's about working as a team."

"Oh, when you do it, you get the credit. When I do it, it's about the team."

"That is not true."

The Extractor

"Uh huh."

"It's not. Now can you stop jacking your jaw long enough for me to get rid of these things?"

Nicole made a sharp turn to her left, causing Bridge to lose his balance. "Go ahead. Who's stopping you?"

Bridge stared at her for a moment, knowing she made that last turn on purpose, wanting him to fall. "Just keep it steady for a minute. Can you do that?"

"Oh, I'll try, sir."

"Sarcasm will get you nowhere."

Nicole slowed down a little bit from her ninety mile an hour speed they were travelling. She also tried to keep the car in as straight a line as she could so Bridge could be accurate with his throws. Bridge climbed onto the edge of the door between the window opening, his back to the outside, his left hand on the roof of the car for support. There were two cars following them, and they weren't far behind. Nicole continued slowing down to give him a better shot at taking them out. After steadying the car for what seemed like forever, Nicole wondered what was taking so long.

"What are you waiting for? You ever gonna throw them things?"

"I gotta make these things count," Bridge shouted back. "I've only got two you know."

"Even if you only get one, I got stuff in the back that will take care of the other one."

"Why does that not surprise me?" Bridge said to himself.

Nicole looked at the speedometer and saw that she was only going fifty. "It's not natural for me to go this slow under these circumstances you know!"

Bridge didn't respond, holding his arm high up over his head, waiting for just the right moment to throw the grenade. He pulled the pin and threw it, the grenade landing on the ground, just in front of the lead car following them, stopping the car immediately as pieces of the car were torn off. The second car sped around the other one, looking like it was gaining speed. Bridge knew he didn't have as long to cue up his shot this time. He grabbed the second grenade and pulled the pin, throwing it at the second car. His aim wasn't as good this time around, but it didn't need to be. It was still effective and got the job done. This time, the grenade exploded as it hit the ground, though the car wasn't immediately affected by the blast. In order to try and avoid the grenade, the driver of the car quickly tried to turn, but was going too fast for such a maneuver, and instead flipped the car over.

Bridge continued sitting between the frame of the window on the door, watching the second car turn over several times. He let out a laugh, pleased with the results.

"Ha ha, that'll teach ya!"

He continued sitting there for another minute, making sure there was nobody else coming. Once Bridge was sure they were no longer being pursued, he slid back down into the car. He looked over at Nicole, a somewhat smug look on his face, happy with his own efforts.

"You gonna apologize now?"

"For what?!" Nicole said.

"For not believing in me. You thought I couldn't get them."

"I never said that."

"You as much as said it."

"I said no such thing!"

"It was written all over your face."

"You're just making things up now."

"Even if you only get one, there's something else in the back. That's what you said."

"I was merely saying we had other options. It was not a reflection of my belief in you being able to get the job done."

"Well, it sounded to me like you were skeptical of my abilities."

"I would never."

"Uh huh. Never out loud maybe."

"You're just trying to start trouble now."

"Now I would never," Bridge said.

"I finish the troubles, remember? I don't start them."

"Well why don't you start thinking about how you're gonna finish this trouble? Rodriguez, Hower, all of that?"

"I'm still thinking about it."

"Well this plan about finding Rodriguez to tell us about Hower didn't go so hot."

"Doesn't mean it's a dud. Just means it…"

"Failed?"

"No."

"Was unsuccessful?"

"No."

"Was terrible?"

"No! Just means it needs to be altered slightly."

"Well, I think you had it right the first time," Nicole said. "I think it's a dud."

"It's not a dud. Not yet."

15

Bridge and Nicole were in their hotel room. Their new hotel room, that is. They weren't comfortable staying in the same room, knowing that Rodriguez had checked Bridge out. So they went to another hotel that was only ten minutes away. It was just as good as their last room and had just as many amenities along with a nice view, which was mostly what Nicole cared about. As Nicole set up her computer equipment again, they started going over their next course of action.

"Rodriguez is still the key," Bridge said.

"You'll never get close to him again."

"We've got to. He's the one who's gonna unwrap this whole thing."

"Like I said, you're not getting close to him again. After everything that happened back there, he's going to be on his guard triply tight."

"Well it's either go after Rodriguez again or forget him and concentrate on Hower directly."

"I think the latter is the way to go. More safe."

"But if we do that, it's going to take a lot longer. Hower and Rodriguez had some type of relationship. We've got proof of that. So if anyone knows what happened to Hower, or knew what, if anything, Hower was into… illegally that is, it's gonna be Rodriguez."

"And as I keep saying, Rodriguez is going to have such tight security from now on, it wouldn't surprise me if he dug himself a hole and stayed there for six months."

"Maybe. But he just lost two cars worth of security, remember."

"But we also don't have me as a surprise anymore," Nicole said. "They now know I'm with you. We're not pulling off any more tricks."

Bridge sat down on the edge of the bed as he thought. "That's true. There must be something else we're overlooking." They both sat in their respective spots, trying to think of an answer. They weren't getting anywhere until it finally occurred to Bridge. "That's it," he said, snapping his fingers.

"What's it?"

"Diego."

"What about him?"

"We dig background on him. Find out where he likes to go, who he likes to hang out with. We use that to find a backdoor into Rodriguez again. We already know Diego's one of his guys."

"And one of his trusted guys, or he wouldn't have sent him to pick you up initially."

Bridge nodded. "That's right."

Nicole immediately turned to her computer and started typing away. "I'll start running him down." After a minute, she suddenly stopped, and looked back at Bridge, who was now looking out the window. "Wait a minute. I just thought of something."

"What's wrong?"

"What if Diego was one of the guys in those cars?"

"Well we don't know the guys in those cars are dead. Even if he was in one of them, he might have gotten out just fine and dandy."

"And if he's not?"

Bridge shrugged. "Then we'll figure out some other way. But even if he is, if we can figure out the places he liked to go, it'll still help."

Nicole went back to her computer and started to try and find out Diego's identity and background.

"How long you think that'll take you?"

Nicole shrugged. "I dunno. Depends how easy it is."

Bridge looked perplexed, thinking that was an odd response. He thought about letting it slide, but just couldn't help himself by replying with something sarcastic. "Well, duh, everything depends on how easy it is. Easy is quick, hard is long. That's kind of self-explanatory isn't it?"

"You know, everything doesn't need to have a witty response."

"Why not?"

Nicole rolled her eyes. "I dunno. Whatever."

Bridge then walked toward the door. "Well, if I'm not back by the time you finish that, call me and let me know, OK?"

"Wait, where are you going?"

"Can't just sit around here all day and wait for something to pop up. Gotta go plant some seeds."

"Seriously?"

"What?"

"You just got done planting some seeds and look where that got you. Almost got both of us killed. And you're gonna go out and do it again."

"You know what they say… early bird catches the worm."

"And how does that apply to this situation?"

Bridge shrugged. "I dunno. Just kind of felt like saying it."

Nicole shook her head. "Exactly what are you going to go do? That way I know if I need to keep my phone and my gun nearby in case I have to come rescue you again." Bridge was about to respond before Nicole put her hand up to stop him. "No, wait, in case I need to extract The Extractor again." Nicole smiled. "There. That was much better."

Bridge faked a smile. "You really enjoy saying that, don't you?"

"Mmm, little bit."

"I shouldn't need any extracting, thank you very much. Instead of looking for Rodriguez, I'm just gonna throw Bill Hower's name around, see if anything pops up."

"Didn't you do that already?"

"I was trying to be discreet the first time though. Now I'm just gonna come right out and ask about him. There's a difference."

"I'm not seeing a difference."

"Well there is one."

"I don't think so."

"Well there is. So that's that, OK?"

"OK. If you wanna go out and waste your time, go right ahead. I'll be right here doing all the real work."

"The real work? Really? Like I'm doing fake stuff out there?"

"I'm not saying anything," Nicole said, typing away. "You go do whatever it is you wanna do."

"I will."

"Good."

"I'll see you when I get back."

"I'll be here."

Bridge then walked out and a few seconds later, Nicole went over to the window to see him walk away from the hotel. Once he was out of sight, she went back to her computer and started digging into Diego. An hour had passed and she wasn't having much luck with it. Instead of continuing to beat her head against the wall, she called Happ, hoping he wasn't in the middle of something important. Thankfully, he answered almost immediately.

"Hey, Eric, hope I didn't pull you away from anything."

"No, no, just pulled me away from a mouth-watering double cheeseburger that I just made myself on the grill."

"Oh. Sorry. That actually sounds really good right now."

"Well the two bites I put into my mouth would agree with you. And those bites are getting lonely, so if you don't mind, I'd like to get back to it as soon as possible."

"Oh. So does that mean you wouldn't be able to help me with something?"

Happ loudly sighed into the phone. He knew what that meant. "Really?"

"Pretty please?" Nicole asked, in her sweetest sounding voice.

Happ knew he was going to get suckered into it. He always did. "Why do you guys do this to me?"

"Because we love you and know we can count on you through even the toughest situations."

"You don't need to pour it on that thick." Happ then took another bite of his cheeseburger. "How important is this, anyway?"

"Could be pretty important."

"How's everything going down there, by the way?"

"Oh, you know, a few explosions here, a few explosions there."

Happ laughed. When he became aware that he was laughing by himself, he realized she might not have been joking. "You're kidding, right?"

"Uhh, sure, let's go with that."

"Are you serious? Are you blowing up the country down there?"

"Not the country. Just a few little cars."

"Do I even need to ask the circumstances?"

"Well we found Rodriguez. And then there was this little thing where Luke got captured and tied up, then I had to rescue him, then there was a little chase once we escaped, then a few grenades were thrown to stop the pursuit, but overall, there wasn't much to it."

"Oh, well, as long as there was nothing to it."

"Yeah, just another day."

"So what was it that you wanted?" Happ asked.

"Oh, umm, one of Rodriguez' associates. A man named Diego. We think he's pretty high up on the food chain and was just wondering if you could help me run him down?"

"You can't do it?"

"Well I've been trying for the last hour and I'm not getting heads or tails over it. I know you guys already have a file on Rodriguez, so I thought maybe you already had a list of all his associates."

"We do. Well, I don't know about all of them, but I know there's a few."

"You think you could take a peek for me?"

"Right now?"

"Well I'm trying to do things the easy way. If not, then I'm gonna have to resort to my bag of tricks."

Happ also knew what that meant. Bridge had already told him enough stories of their exploits that Happ knew Nicole's reputation as well. "No, let's not do that. There's already been enough things exploding since you've been there."

"I'd really appreciate it."

"When do you need it by?"

"Uhh, well, within the hour would be really really helpful."

"Seriously? I've worked late every night for the last two weeks, and the one night I actually get home on time, and am able to cook a decent dinner, I'm still gonna wind up working?"

"Uhhh… I love you?"

Happ sighed. Being nice did have an effect on him, as much as he hated it. "You better not let my wife hear you say that?"

"Oh, your wife's heard me say that to you a hundred times."

"You're lucky she went out with the kids for an hour."

"You're finally home on time and she went out?"

"Playground date with one of the kid's friends from school."

"Oh. Well see, what else were you gonna do?"

"I could think of about fifty things."

"It would really be helpful," Nicole said. "I'll owe you one."

Happ laughed. "You owe me about twenty already that I'm sure I'll never get paid back for."

"I promise you'll get paid back with interest."

"I'd love to see how that would work."

"You know I wouldn't call unless I really needed you."

Happ sighed again. "Yeah, I know. All right, I'll do some digging, but only until my wife gets home. If I haven't found out anything by then it'll have to wait until I get to the office tomorrow morning."

"Deal."

"OK. I'll call you in an hour if I find anything."

Not wanting to just sit around and wait for Happ's call, Nicole continued trying to find out whatever she could on her own. It was tough sledding though. There just wasn't much out there on Diego. About forty-five minutes later, Nicole's phone rang.

"Hey, you're fifteen minutes early."

"What do you expect from the best?" Happ said with a laugh.

"Does that mean you've got something? Or did your wife come home early?"

"Diego Sanchez, twenty-four years old, I'm sending a picture to your email now. Let me know if this is the guy."

Nicole quickly pulled up her email and downloaded

the file that Happ sent over. "Yep. That's him. What do you have on him?"

"Local guy, been arrested for minor things over the years. His first pickup was at fifteen. Been in trouble ever since."

"Sounds about right."

"Never been to the States as far as I can tell so we don't have a ton on him, but he is listed as a known associate of Rodriguez."

"What about hangouts? Got anything?"

"Uhh, only thing I could really come up with was a club named El Gran Azul. At least I think it's a club."

"The Big Blue? What kind of name is that?"

"I dunno. I think because it's painted blue on the outside and the walls inside are blue too, something like that. Anyway, I found out he's been picked up twice there over the years, so if you're looking for him, there's a good chance he might be there at some point."

"All right, good, thanks. You got anything else?"

"No, that's pretty much it. Seems like he's pretty small-time so there's not a whole lot out there on him."

"Well, this should be good enough to start with. Thanks, Eric, I owe you one."

"Where have I heard that before?"

Nicole laughed. "Yeah, anyway, enjoy the rest of your night. Don't take any more phone calls involving work."

"Turning my phone off the minute I hang up."

After putting her phone down, Nicole immediately

The Extractor

started looking up the club that Diego was known to frequent. Luckily there were pictures on the internet of it. Happ wasn't kidding when he said it was called that because it was painted blue. It really was. But it did help the building stand out. The outside was a dark blue building, while the inside walls were painted light blue, and even had strips of neon blue lights that went throughout the building. They even had blue strobe lights periodically set up.

"Man, that really is blue, isn't it?" Nicole said to herself.

The more Nicole looked up information on the building, the more she saw that it was increasingly becoming a popular spot among locals and tourists. It was basically just a regular night club with drinking, dancing, and music. She couldn't wait to tell Bridge about it when he got back. She knew he'd be thrilled about going there. Actually, she knew he'd hate it. He always hated going to clubs and other hip spots. He was thirty-three but sometimes acted like he was a grumpy old man when it came to visiting places like that. He always complained that he was getting too old to go to businesses like that, said it was for younger people, as if he were too old. But it was one more chance for Nicole to get him riled up, which she enjoyed.

It was about two hours later when Bridge finally walked through the door. He looked tired and had an expression on his face that indicated he didn't make out too well with whatever he was doing. Nicole knew the news she had to share would make him happy at first, until he found out where they'd be going. She got herself mentally ready to hear the whining he was about to spew out.

Nicole stopped typing to turn to the side and face him. "Looks like you've had a rough time."

"I feel like I've gone to half the bars in Mexico."

"How many did you hit?"

"I don't know. I stopped counting after thirty."

"Well did you find out anything?"

"Not a thing," Bridge said, sitting down on the edge of the bed. He looked exhausted as he took his shoes off.

"Good."

Bridge scrunched his eyebrows together as he looked at her curiously. "Why is it good that I came up empty?"

"Because I didn't."

"You got something?"

"Of course. You really expected me to fail?"

"Well…"

"Gee, thanks."

"So what'd you get?"

"Just that Diego's last name is Sanchez and he likes to visit a place called El Gran Azul."

Bridge looked down at the floor. "The Big Blue? What kind of name is that?"

Nicole laughed. "That's exactly what I said. Kind of scary we're thinking alike nowadays, huh?"

"You have no idea."

"Anyway, I've already looked the place up, so get yourself rested for a few hours so we can head there later."

"What do you mean, rest up so we can head there later? What kind of place is this?"

"Oh, I dunno. Just a bar type place."

"A bar type place?" Bridge thought about it for a few more seconds. He could tell by the gleeful look on Nicole's face that there was more to the story. She was leaving something out. "Wait a minute. This is a club, isn't it?"

A wide smile came over Nicole's face. "Sure is. Music, dancing and drinking, looks like we'll have to put on the old couple act once again."

Bridge's shoulders slumped, not really in the mood for that type of scene. "No, why does it have to be a club?"

Nicole shrugged. "I dunno. Just the kind of place that Diego likes to go I guess."

"But why a club?" Bridge whined.

"What's the matter with clubs?"

"Clubs are for young people to have fun. It's no kind of place for people like me."

"Luke, you're thirty-three years old. Stop talking like you're an old man or something."

"I am an old man." Bridge then pointed to his chest. "In here."

Nicole rolled her eyes. "You'll be fine. There are

plenty of people in their thirties, and even forties, who go to clubs."

"Yeah, but they're, like… different," Bridge said, waving his hand in the air, not knowing how to reinforce his point. He then let his body fall back onto the bed and looked up at the ceiling. "I hate clubs!"

"What's your exact issue with them? Other than your age."

"Because they're loud and noisy and have way too many people there. It's hard to concentrate, hard to spot people, hard to follow people once you've spotted them, and there's just too much going on."

"There might be some good looking women there."

"It's not even worth it." Bridge then sat back up. "Especially with you there to scare them all away."

"I would not scare them all away. Probably."

"Uh huh. You got pictures of this dump?"

"It is not a dump." Nicole then brought her laptop over to the bed and started showing him the pictures of it."

"Oh my god, it's even worse than I imagined."

"It's not that bad. It's a nice looking place. I hear it's very popular."

"Oh great, it's gonna be jam-packed. The news just keeps getting worse."

"I think you're overexaggerating just a little bit."

"I am not." Nicole took her laptop back to the desk as Bridge tried to shake the images of blue walls out of his head. "How'd you find this place anyway?"

"Hmm?" Nicole said, not wanting to admit she had Happ's help."

"I said how did you come across this place?"

"Oh, you know, just did some digging."

"Yeah, but how? What'd you dig into?"

"Just the usual stuff."

Bridge thought she was being very vague, which was unlike her. She usually didn't have any problems telling him how she got information. Whenever she replied with generic answers, she was trying to hide something from him. After tossing a few more questions at her, he measured her answers carefully. There was no doubt in his mind she was evading the topic. After thinking about it for a minute, he came up with the answer on his own.

"You talked to Eric, didn't you?"

"What?"

Bridge smiled and laughed, knowing he'd hit on it. "You did. You called Eric and had him run it down for you while I was out."

"I did no such thing."

"That's how you found all this out. You struck out and couldn't find anything so you got desperate and said a few sweet things to Eric to get him to do your dirty work, didn't you?"

"I don't know what you're talking about. You can even call Eric right now and ask him. Go ahead, call him. You'll find that he won't pick up."

"How would you know that unless you called?"

Nicole put the tip of her finger in her mouth. "Uhh, just a lucky guess. I actually don't know if he'll pick up or not."

Bridge squinted his eyes as he looked at her, getting a clear picture of what happened in his mind. "I know what happened."

"You do?"

"You called him, he gave you the stuff, then he turned his phone off, didn't he?"

"Pfft, no. Of course not. Why would you think that?"

"That's it, isn't it? Just admit that's what happened."

"I'll do no such thing."

"Just admit it. I'll keep bothering you about it until you do. You know I will."

"All right, fine, I called him. Happy now?"

"Actually… yes." Bridge shook his head. "Shameful. Making it seem like you did all the work."

"Well I did do the work. I just didn't find anything. I've been looking up information about this club though."

"Oh, don't remind me about it."

"Well you better get used to it, Slick, 'cause we're going there in a few hours. Get some sleep now if you want it."

Bridge sighed. "You really know how to kick a guy when he's down, don't you?"

"It won't be that bad. Who knows, you might even have some fun."

"Don't talk such nonsense. I guarantee there will be no fun had there tonight by anybody in this room. Especially me."

"Woohoo, clubbing here we come!"

Bridge lay face first on the bed, burying his head in the pillow. "Ugh. Torture. Send me back to Rodriguez' place."

16

Bridge opened his eyes upon feeling the slight shake of his shoulder. His eyes flickered as he looked up at the ceiling. For a few moments, he wasn't sure where he was, though he quickly remembered. He was in one of those deep sleeps where a person wakes up and just can't remember anything at first. But it only lasted a few seconds. He looked up and saw Nicole's pretty, smiling face, then looked over at the window, seeing that it was night time. He sat up, still looking kind of groggy.

"What time is it?"

Nicole smiled. "Time to go clubbing."

"Oh no," Bridge said, laying back down. "Let me go back to bed."

"No, no, no, you know we have to do this." Nicole grabbed his arm and started lifting him back up. Bridge could have tried to fight it, but knew there was no point. Nicole could be relentless sometimes, especially when she already had it in her mind that they were going to do something. In most cases, that meant they were going to do it, regardless of how much he tried to fight.

"Why?"

"We've already been over this."

"Why don't you just go on your own?"

"Really?"

"Sure. I mean, you're attractive enough, you can handle yourself, you fit in there more than I do."

"You're really gonna send me in there all alone to possibly face a violent criminal and any pals he might bring? Me? I'll be vulnerable, weak, defenseless…"

Bridge started laughing. "Are you kidding? You? Vulnerable, weak, and defenseless? There's a lot of things you could be called, Nic, but one of those things is not it. You are anything but any of those. You only start saying that type of stuff when you're trying to pour on the guilt and make me go somewhere."

"Is it working?"

"No. I'm tired. Just let me stay here and sleep."

Nicole really wasn't going to take no for an answer and she wasn't pussyfooting around anymore. "Luke, c'mon, let's go! Stop acting like a baby and put your big boy pants on. We all have to do things we don't like sometimes, so stop your nonsense. We're doing this for a case, remember, not just because we want to go out and shake our bon-bon's."

Bridge sighed. He hated it when she poured it on thick like that. He hated it even more when she was right. He grunted for a moment, then picked himself off the bed and stood up. "Fine. Let's go."

"We can't."

"What? You just said…"

"I know what I said. But you can't go. Not looking like that. You have to change into something more appropriate."

Bridge's mouth fell open as he looked at the ceiling. "This is why I hate this stuff. Not only do I have to go somewhere I don't want to go, now I also have to change to do it."

Nicole shrugged. "Well you just can't roll into a popular night hotspot looking like you just rolled out of bed after digging ditches for twelve hours. You have to look like you belong."

"But I don't belong."

"Well, you will tonight."

"What about you?" Bridge asked, observing his partner in shorts and a t-shirt.

Nicole looked at herself. "What about me?"

"Doesn't exactly look like you belong out on the dance floor shaking your booty to DJ Jazzy Whoever wearing that."

"I'm obviously going to change."

"Oh, obviously. Wasn't obvious to me."

Nicole rolled her eyes and shook her head, as she often did at something he said. "If you want to get dressed, then I will too."

"Oh. OK. Who gets changed where?"

"You stay out here. I get the bathroom."

"Why do you get the bathroom?"

"Women need more time."

"Boy, ain't that the truth."

Nicole then grabbed a small bag off the chair by the table and went into the bathroom to change, while Bridge went into his suitcase and removed some clothes that would work. He changed into a nice pair of pants with a button down shirt with some black shoes. It took him less than ten minutes to be ready. As he looked in the mirror to make sure he was presentable, he looked over at the bathroom door, noticing that his partner still wasn't out yet. He went over to it and knocked on the door.

"Almost done?"

"Few more minutes," Nicole replied.

Bridge sighed. "Yeah, few more meaning thirty probably."

"What'd you say?"

"Nothing. I said I'll just wait here until you're done."

"OK."

Bridge grabbed a soda can out of the refrigerator as he waited, then sat down on the edge of the bed. He actually wound up waiting about ten more minutes before Nicole finally sauntered out of the bathroom. He casually glanced at her as she emerged from the bathroom, not really expecting much, at least nothing that he hadn't seen before. But she had really outdone herself this time. Holding the can a few inches from his face, Bridge felt like he was paralyzed watching her, only moving his eyes as he couldn't take them off his partner. She was wearing a one piece dress, the top of which revealed quite a bit of her cleavage, and the bottom of which barely went halfway down her thigh. And it was tight. It looked to Bridge like she was about to burst out of it any minute. But he couldn't look away. He couldn't do anything, other than stare.

Knowing he was ogling, he took his eyes away and focused on the soda can, though he still didn't move his arm. He then looked back at Nicole again, before returning them back to the can. He finally was able to move again, taking the last remaining sip left from the can. After briefly looking at Nicole again, he opened his eyes wide again, as if he had just gotten out of bed and was trying to wake himself up. Nicole walked around the room, knowing what kind of effect she was having on him. She glanced at him a few times, seeing him stare at her like he was. And she liked it. It wasn't often that he looked at her that way, not often enough in her mind. It just reinforced in her own mind that there really was something there between them. Maybe looking like that a few more times would finally drop that wall that he put up between them and actually do what she wanted him to do. Wanting to tease him a little bit more, Nicole stood right in front of him so he could get a good view.

"Do I look OK?"

Bridge looked her up and down, though was careful not to let his eyes linger and stare this time. "Uhh, yeah, yeah, you look fine."

"Just fine?"

"Umm... great, I guess?"

"You guess? Do I look terrible or something?"

"Uhh, no, no, you don't... it's just..."

"It's just what?"

"Well, I'm not used to seeing you like that."

"Like what?"

Bridge waved his arm at her, then up and down, not really knowing what he was doing with it. "You know... like that. Like, all done up and all."

"So I look bad?"

"No, no, you just look beau... well, you know, you look... like you're going clubbing."

"Then I look OK for where we're going then?"

"Umm, yeah, yeah, yep. Just... yep." Bridge then itched his head, a little uncomfortable with this entire conversation.

Nicole smiled, knowing she was getting him all tongue-twisted. "You look very handsome yourself."

"Oh, thanks. Yeah, not nearly as good as you, but, uhh... yeah. You might not, uhh, be able to do much work while we're there though."

"Why not?"

Bridge then started waving his hand at her again. "Well, you know, looking like that... you might be... distracted."

"Why would I be distracted?"

"Well, I mean, not you per se, but, you know, there's probably going to be a lot of guys who are looking at you and try to… you know… flirt or dance or something. You'll be, uhh, distracted because they're distracted."

Nicole smiled again, enjoying the fact that he seemed so uncomposed. It was something she didn't see often in him. "And what about you? You won't be distracted or anything with me looking like this? 'Cause I wouldn't want to have that effect on you and distract you from our mission."

"What, me? No, no, no need to worry about that. I am, uhh, I will be totally focused on everything else, yeah. No, uhh, yeah, I'm good." Bridge then continued looking at her dress, along with her in it. It certainly showed off her frame in a good way in his view. "Where did you get that, by the way? I don't remember ever seeing that before."

"Oh, that's because I just got it. I didn't really bring anything with me that would be appropriate for the club, so while you were sleeping, I just went to the store and grabbed something. It was like the first thing I saw, and I wasn't even sure it was my style, it was just something quick and easy that I picked out. I didn't put any effort or second thought into it at all."

"Oh. Well it certainly looks… uhh, yeah, I'd say that we're ready then, I guess. Don't you?"

"Yeah, I would say so."

Before leaving, Nicole took the opportunity to tease him a little bit more. She turned around, giving him ample opportunity to see every side of her.

"Before we go, you're sure I look OK?"

"You look..." Bridge couldn't even finish his thought. He just gave her the OK sign with his thumb and index finger.

"It's not too much or anything? I don't want to look out of place."

"Believe me, you will not look out of place. You might not leave there alive though."

"What do you mean?"

"Because the looks you'll be getting from some of the other women there, if looks could kill, you probably would get murdered. They'll be so jealous that you're stealing the eyes of the guys and their boyfriends there..." Bridge realized he started staring at her again and even had a slight smile on his face as he was doing it. He quickly regained his stoic expression, not wanting to give the impression that he was even remotely interested in Nicole in any romantic fashion whatsoever, even though he probably wouldn't have resisted her if she had come onto him at that moment.

A huge smile came over Nicole's face, happy that he was actually seeing her in a different light for a change. "Why thank you. You know, that might be the best compliment you've ever given me."

"I've given you lots of compliments before."

"Usually for what I do, but not for me and how I look."

"You know how you look."

"But you never really tell me."

"I didn't think I needed to."

"It'd be nice to hear sometimes."

The conversation was getting heavy, too heavy for Bridge's tastes, and he could tell it was starting to go down a road that he didn't want to go, at least not right now.

"I guess we should be going now, huh?"

Nicole looked slightly disappointed at first, secretly hoping that he would spill out some reserved feelings he had built up for her. With that not coming, she quickly picked her spirits back up and walked out of the room, immediately followed by Bridge. As they walked down the hallway to the elevator, Nicole flirtily flicked at his shirt collar.

"Time to go clubbin'."

The disdain that Bridge showed on his face was clearly evident. The fact of where they were going was only slightly improved by the fact he got to look at a beautiful woman by his side for the rest of the night. "It sure is."

17

Bridge and Nicole started walking toward the club and let a few people pass them on the street as they looked up at the building.

"That sure is blue, isn't it?" Bridge said.

"It's not that blue. I mean, it's blue, but not that blue."

"It's like a medium blue. Not dark, dark blue, but not a light, or baby blue either. It's like a neutral blue. It's actually not as blue as I pictured in my mind."

"Well you saw the pictures. You knew how blue it was."

"Yeah, but the blue in the pictures looked different than the blue here. It's actually not a bad blue. It's just blue enough to be not an overpowering blue or too soft a blue. It's just right."

Nicole turned her head and glared at him, knowing he was just having fun with all the blue talk. It was actually him stalling, trying to think of anything to avoid going in.

"Are you done now?"

"Done what?" Bridge innocently asked.

"All this stupid blue talk. The building's blue. We don't need to analyze it for an hour before going in."

"I wasn't analyzing it. I was just…"

"Yeah, yeah, I know what you were doing. Let's just go."

Nicole grabbed Bridge's arm and spun him around to get him walking in the right direction. Within a minute they were lined up at the front door. Nicole periodically looked at Bridge's face as they waited to get in, and could tell his anxiety was kicking in. She didn't know what it was, or why he got so nervous about clubs, but she could see the perspiration forming on his forehead. Maybe like when he was in Mexico, maybe he had a bad experience in a club one time. That was the only thing Nicole could figure. It couldn't have simply been that he didn't like clubs. Nothing was ever that simple with Bridge. With anything he didn't like, there was always a story behind it. She just hadn't hit on it yet.

"Are you OK?"

"Hmm? Yeah, I'm fine, I'm fine."

"You look like you're about to pass out or something."

"I'm good," Bridge replied.

"OK. Well, if you're not, just focus on something until we get inside"

Bridge looked at the front of the line, seeing they still had what seemed like forever to go. He took a deep breath and tried to relax, though it didn't seem to be helping. He thought of Nicole's words and looked around to focus on something, though he didn't come up with anything until his eyes happened to glance at the beautiful woman in front of him. He had no problem focusing on the back of Nicole's dress, or more importantly, the woman inside it. He didn't know what it was, but since seeing her put that dress on, he was getting some lustful feelings inside. It was actually starting to scare him a little. After a few minutes, and as they got closer, Nicole turned around and grabbed her partner's hands and put them on her waist.

"We're supposed to be a couple. We should start doing couple-like things."

Bridge closed his eyes, knowing this maneuver wasn't going to do anything to help quench those feelings he'd been having. This would only make them worse. He couldn't deny, though, that it did feel nice. Not only having his hands on her body, but just the feeling in general, of being with someone, was a change from his usual interactions with women. He couldn't even remember the last time he was in a relationship with someone. Ever since joining the CIA, it was casual flings, one-night stands, and occasionally someone who'd stick around for a few months, but no permanent commitments. Bridge cared for some of them, but never enough for anything more to grow out of that relationship. He just didn't think he was the type of guy who would commit to one person for the rest of his life. Or maybe it was just his job and the lifestyle he led that infiltrated the back of his mind, not wanting to make a widow out of whoever he was tied down with, knowing that the job was dangerous and could take him out at any time.

It was only a few more minutes before Bridge and Nicole finally got through the front door. Once inside, they took a quick look around to see where all the action was. To their left was the bar area with some seating, and to the right was the dance floor, though there were also some steps toward the middle, though there was another guard stationed at the bottom, with a rope going across to prevent any unwelcomed guests going up. They were so focused on scouting their surroundings that Bridge didn't even notice he still had his one hand wrapped around Nicole's waist. She noticed, though, but didn't mind.

"What do you think's going on upstairs?" Nicole asked.

"I'd say that's for the VIP's."

"I wonder how you get up there?"

"Probably need an invitation."

"Wonder if Diego's up there."

"Problem is we won't know unless we see him go up."

"We'll need a good view of these steps at all times."

"Yeah."

Bridge looked around for a good spot, noticing an empty table near the bar that looked like it was a good spot. They went over to it and sat down and immediately made sure they could still see the stairs from there. They could, though with all the patrons in the building coming and going, they would still have to look around all the people there.

"Hope he's not up there already," Nicole said.

"I doubt it. I mean, what would be the odds of him being here the moment we walk in the building, and the first time that we're here? Probably astronomical."

"Still, could happen."

"We could be here for a week and never see him," Bridge said. "He might not ever come back here again."

Nicole shook her head. "The information suggests he likes this place. He's been busted here several times. That means he's not afraid of people knowing he's here if he does that. That means he really likes it here. He's not giving it up unless he moves out of the area."

Bridge nodded, acknowledging that made sense. "Just a question of how long we're waiting."

"Might as well get some drinks to pass the time."

Bridge nodded again, getting up to order themselves a little something to keep them company. As he was waiting at the bar for their drinks, he happened to look back at the table, and saw another man sitting at his seat.

"Well that didn't take long."

Bridge figured men would be looking at Nicole, but he didn't think someone would take his seat less than ten seconds after getting up. He noticed Nicole smiling as she talked to the man and it started to make Bridge a little jealous. He didn't like another man talking to her. Or maybe it was the fact that she had a smile on her face as she talked to him. Either way, it was a new feeling for him. Bridge shook his head and turned his head back to the bar so he wouldn't look at them, trying not to let it bother him.

"What are you doing?" Bridge said to himself. "Why are you letting this get to you? You're not involved, you're not in a relationship, just let it go."

The bartender then came back with their drinks. Bridge turned around to look at the table again, and he was shocked to see a different man at the table now.

"I guess the other guy got replaced."

Bridge waited there for a second with their drinks in his hands, waiting for the man to move on. He cleared his throat, becoming increasingly annoyed at the attention Nicole seemed to be getting.

"Stop it, stop it, stop it. Do not get jealous. I just... I already talked to you about this, you're not involved. Just let it go and move on."

Bridge continued waiting by the bar, waiting for the man to move on. After a minute, his annoyance was growing ever longer, as it seemed Nicole was enjoying the conversation by the smile on her face. His attention was briefly diverted when an attractive woman, also not wearing much, walked over to him. She gave him a seductive smile. He scarcely paid her any mind.

"Are one of those drinks for me?"

Bridge barely looked at her, trying to keep his focus on the table. "Huh? No, they're for... someone else."

"Oh. Well, maybe you and I could go to a quieter part of the room?"

"No, I'm OK, thank you."

"I'm here visiting from California. What about you?"

"Business."

"Oh. What business are you in?"

"Excuse me, I can't stand here any longer."

Bridge walked past the blonde, making a beeline for Nicole's table. He put an angry expression on his face, trying to play the part of the jealous boyfriend, though in truth, he really didn't have to act all that much. Once he got to the table, he angrily slammed the drinks down, looking at the man sitting in his seat.

"You messing with my girlfriend?"

The man looked up at him, stunned, then stumbled off the chair. "No, no, I didn't realize you were together."

"Well we came in together. What, I leave for two seconds and you think it's mating season or something?"

The man continued to backtrack, putting his hands in the air, not wanting a confrontation. "I'm really sorry, man, I didn't know she was taken."

"Well she is."

"Wouldn't try to steal her away. I apologize. My fault. No harm, no foul."

Bridge nodded, realizing his act worked. "All right then."

"We good?"

"Yeah, we're good," Bridge said, sitting down. "By the way, there's a blonde at the bar from California. She's looking for someone. Might wanna check her out."

The man smiled, appreciating the tip. "Thanks, man, I'll have a go at it."

As the man walked past him, Bridge took a sip of his drink, not looking at Nicole. He didn't have to look at her to know she was staring at him. He could feel it. She kept smiling at him, wondering when he was going to stop pretending he was focusing on something else and look at her. After about thirty seconds, Bridge's eyes briefly glanced at her.

"That was a really good performance you put on, pretending you were my boyfriend and all."

"Gotta play the part, right?"

"Almost seemed like you were really mad."

A sour-looking face came over Bridge. "What? Don't be ridiculous. Just part of the performance."

"Oh. So you weren't really mad?"

"No. Of course not. Why would I be mad?"

"I don't know."

"I mean, just because I was gone for like three

minutes and you had two guys here keeping my seat warm for me."

Nicole started a smile, realizing he was a bit jealous, but quickly wiped it away. "Yeah, I was surprised too, they just came up and started flirting with me. I was about to send the other guy away when you came back anyway."

"Oh really? Judging by the smile on your face you seemed to be enjoying the attention from both of them."

"Well I didn't want to be rude and shut them down right away. They both seemed nice and respectful, and it takes courage to approach someone like that, so I was just trying to be nice."

"Oh, is that what it was?" Bridge said. "Nice. Huh. Looked to me like if I didn't come back to the table that you wouldn't have missed me."

Nicole leaned on the table and put her hand over her mouth to prevent herself from laughing. She was finding his demeanor humorous. He was mad and jealous without even realizing it.

"Well it's not like I have a real boyfriend or anything, so it's not like there's anything preventing me from enjoying a conversation with someone, right?"

"I guess not," Bridge said, looking toward the VIP steps.

Nicole took a sip from her drink. "Luke, are you jealous that a couple of men were talking to me?"

Bridge snapped his head back to look at her. "What? No. Absolutely not. No. That's crazy."

"Because it seems like you are." Nicole then put her thumb and finger in the air, slightly apart from each other. "Just a little bit."

"That's ridiculous. I'm not jealous. Why would I be? Over what?"

Nicole shrugged. "I don't know. Just seemed like you are."

"Well I'm not. Just wanna make sure you're focused on the mission and not flirting with all the Don Juan's in here."

"I'm focused. Are you focused."

"I'm focused."

"Good. I guess we're all focused then."

Bridge couldn't help but glance at her chest as he looked back to the steps again, really hoping Diego would show up soon. Even though he said otherwise, he was as unfocused as he'd ever been. "Yep, all focused."

18

THEY'D BEEN at the club for five days straight, with still no sign of Diego. Somehow, they managed to secure the same table for four of those days. Bridge was lucky in that he wasn't taunted by Nicole's dress all week, though she had it on again tonight. At least she wore more conservative clothing the past few days. It didn't seem to stop the number of men trying to make a pass at her though. Every night they'd been there, Bridge had to shoo men away from the table. There were even two nights that Nicole was somehow able to drag Bridge onto the dance floor, and Bridge had to even brush people away from cutting in there too.

As far as Bridge was concerned, this was a nightmare assignment. Every day at the hotel, he especially, tried to think of other ways to get the information they wanted. Going back to that club every night was like hell for him. Nicole, on the other hand, didn't mind the job so much. They basically got to have fun, at least in her mind, until Diego showed up. And there was no question in her mind that Diego was going to show up. Bridge was not so sure. But without any other leads to go on, he reluctantly kept agreeing to go back to the club.

"You know, maybe we're going about this all wrong," Bridge said.

"What do you mean?"

"Maybe we shouldn't be going after Diego or Rodriguez at all. Maybe we need to dig deeper somewhere else."

Nicole laughed. "You're only saying that 'cause you don't want to be here."

"No, besides that. I mean, how long are we going to sit here and wait for someone who may or may not show up? We have to admit the possibility Diego might never come here. I think it's time we moved on and looked for other ways to find out what happened to Hower. I mean, somebody must know something."

"Someone does. Rodriguez."

"I mean besides him."

"I say we give it two more days. Then if he doesn't show, we can say we gave it a solid week."

Bridge closed his eyes, sighed, and slumped his shoulders. Nicole saying two more days, she might as well have been saying the rest of their lives, because that's what it felt like to him. Nicole smiled at him as he went through his gyrations.

"This is really torture for you, isn't it?"

"You have no idea."

"What bothers you so much?"

"We've already had this conversation before," Bridge said. "It's all of it. All of it. There's not one bit of this that I like."

"Not one?"

Bridge glanced down at some of Nicole's exposed skin and had to rethink his statement. "Well, most of it anyway." He then put his elbow on the table to rest his head as he looked away, not wanting to stare at her again. "And I'm tired of telling Mrs. Hower the same thing. I've talked to her two times this past week, both saying the same thing. I'm tired of saying I got nothing."

"These things take time, Luke, you know that. How many jobs have we been on when it was wrapped up in just a few days? Not many."

"Not enough."

"This is just part of the deal."

"Doesn't mean I have to be ecstatic about it."

A taller gentleman, looking to be in his late twenties, then approached the table. He had slicked back hair, an athletic looking build, and wasn't too bad looking.

"Excuse me, I've been watching you for a while and was wondering if I may have a dance with this beautiful lady here?"

Nicole looked up at him and smiled. Bridge did not have the same reaction.

"That's my girlfriend, man, get lost."

The man put his arms up. "Hey, no offense meant. Wasn't trying to steal her away or anything."

Bridge stood up. "That's exactly what you were trying to do." Bridge reached his hand across his waist, insinuating that he may have been packing a weapon. "Better get lost or you're gonna have a bigger problem on your hands."

The man instantly retreated into a crowd, out of Bridge's sight. As soon as he sat down, he noticed Nicole staring at him.

"What?"

"I can't believe you did that."

"What, you wanted to dance with that crumb?"

"No, that you pretended you have a gun."

"Who's pretending?"

"You got a weapon through security?"

Bridge shrugged like it was no big deal. "Doesn't everybody?"

Nicole put her hand on her head. "Oh my gosh, you're gonna get us in trouble. What if he goes and tells someone?"

"He wouldn't dare. Besides, what's he gonna say, I put my hand on my pants? He'll sound like a crazy person. See, this is what happens when I'm in this kind of place for too long. I mean, you're partly to blame."

"Me?! How's it my fault?!"

"Well you're the one that brought me here. This was your plan."

"So it's my fault that you're starting to go nuts?!"

"Yeah." Nicole was more than a little irritated and stood up. "Where are you going?"

"I'm going to go and enjoy myself. Which I should be able to do as long as I'm not near you."

Nicole stormed off, heading towards the dance floor.

"We're supposed to be here on business, you know," Bridge said. He looked around to make sure he wasn't speaking too loudly, but nobody seemed to be paying him any attention, Nicole included.

Bridge looked at the bar for a minute or two, then let his eyes drift back to the dance floor. He immediately picked Nicole out. She wasn't hard to miss with that dress on. He was a little angry that she seemed to be dancing with another man though. Bridge stood up, ready to go over there and put a stop to it, though he looked around and decided to sit back down. A few minutes later, she was dancing with another guy. Bridge couldn't be sure, but he was sure that she was deliberately remaining in plain view of him, trying to rub it in. He clasped his hands together and put them in front of his face as he stared straight ahead, trying not to pay her any attention. After a few minutes, Bridge happened to look over again and saw Nicole dancing with a third guy.

"Oh, this is ridiculous. You're doing that deliberately," Bridge said, even though she couldn't hear him.

Bridge was sitting by himself for about twenty minutes until Nicole came back.

"Are you happy now?"

"About what?" Nicole replied.

"We're supposed to be here on a mission and you're off over there shaking your booty all over the place."

"I was not shaking my booty all over the place."

"That's not what I saw."

"Excuse me?"

"I mean, did you really need to rub up against every single man on the dance floor."

"Really, Luke? I mean, really?"

"You're the one doing it."

"I danced with three or four guys. That's hardly every single man in here."

"Seemed to be enjoying it a lot."

"There's nothing wrong with having a good time."

"Except we're not here for a good time. We're supposed to be on business. Not flaunting ourselves all over the place."

"I am not flaunting myself."

Bridge looked at her body and raised his eyebrows. "That's not what I'm seeing."

"What?" Nicole looked down at her dress. "You said I looked fine in this. Now you're saying I'm flaunting? Are you changing your opinion?"

"Maybe."

"So what's your problem? The fact that I was dancing, the dress, what?"

"All of it. Can we just drop it now and get back to business?"

"Diego's not here yet, we don't have any business to get back to. And no, we're not dropping it. What exactly is your problem? What, you don't like me dancing with other men? Is that it?"

Bridge looked away and took a deep breath, not really wanting to get into it. But he knew Nicole was not going to just drop it. Not unless Diego suddenly walked into the building.

"So what is it, Luke? Is it that I'm revealing too much? Is it the dancing with other men? What is it?"

Bridge stayed silent for a few moments, but eventually burst out with it. "It's all of it, OK? I don't like any of it."

"Oh, so you don't like this dress?"

Bridge looked at her and couldn't truthfully say that he didn't. He couldn't even lie about it. "Well, no, it's not that, it's…"

"It's what?"

"It's just...it's, it's… it's… it's complicated, all right?"

"So uncomplicate it. What don't you like about me in this dress?"

"Nothing. There's nothing I don't like about you in that dress. You look sexy, and beautiful, and amazing, and all of that, OK?"

"So what is the problem? You just don't want to see me with another guy? Is that it? Are you jealous?"

"What? Me? Jealous? Don't be ridiculous. I'm not a bit jealous."

"Well if you're not jealous, then why would it bother you?"

"Because… because we're supposed to be on a job right now."

"But the job's not here."

"But it could be," Bridge said. "And you wouldn't know that if you're dancing away your bon-bon."

"I can still see the steps from the dance floor."

"I have my doubts about that."

Nicole sat back and folded her arms. "You're jealous. That's what this is all about. You're jealous."

"Let's not start that again. I am not jealous. I am so far away from jealous I'm… unjealous." Bridge looked down at the table and made a strange face, knowing he didn't say that as good as he wanted to, but whatever. He just let it be.

"Oh, you are so jealous. I can tell. You don't want other guys being with me. Just admit it."

"I am not admitting anything. Can we just drop this please so we can concentrate?"

"On what? The air? I think we can talk and look at the same time."

"It's more difficult."

"No, you just want to try and get out of talking about this."

"About what?"

"Your feelings," Nicole said. "Admit it, you've got some."

"I do not. And I don't have to admit anything."

"Yes you do."

"I do not. Can we just drop this whole conversation please?"

"Why? Is it making you uncomfortable? Afraid you might actually admit something you don't want to?"

"No, none of that! I just want to talk about something else."

"Like what?"

"Diego," Bridge said, observing the man walk through the front doors.

"Please, what else can we say about him? You're just trying to change the subject."

"No, I mean, Diego. He's here. He's standing right there."

Nicole spun her head around, seeing their target by the front door, greeting a few friends. "Oh my gosh. I can't believe it. He's actually here."

"You say that like you didn't think he'd show up."

"Well, truth be told, I did have my doubts. I just wasn't going to admit it to you. Should we duck so he doesn't see us?"

"Doesn't seem like he's much interested in looking this way."

After Diego greeted his friends near the door, he went up the steps. As he disappeared onto the second floor, Bridge and Nicole came up with a new plan.

"Should we go up and grab him?"

Bridge looked around. "Considering it looks like

he's got friends here, I'm not sure grabbing him is the best idea. Might have to fight our way out of here."

"So we wait."

"We wait."

"As long as we're waiting, you mind if I go back on the dance floor again?" Nicole asked, finding torturing her partner somewhat amusing.

Judging by Bridge's reaction though, he wasn't amused. "You sit right there and don't move."

"So we're back to waiting here again?"

"We're back to waiting here… again."

19

Not knowing how long Diego was planning on staying at the club, Bridge and Nicole quickly had to decide how they were going to talk to him. Doing it there at the club was too risky since it seemed he had friends there. They either had to grab him outside somewhere after he left or follow him to wherever he was going next. With that in mind, it was decided that Nicole would stay in the club while Bridge waited outside. They originally flip-flopped it, because Bridge didn't really want Nicole in the club by herself, knowing she would probably get hit on by half a dozen guys at least while she was in there alone, but Bridge didn't want her waiting outside looking like that either. And while he knew she could handle herself in most cases, he didn't want to worry about her being outside alone, looking as attractive as she was. At least in the club he didn't have to worry about her safety with all the people around.

They each put earpieces in so they could still communicate with each other, not wanting to constantly be on the phone. They hoped they would have a short wait, wanting to get it over with as quickly as possible, especially Bridge, who at this point just wanted to get as far away from this club as possible. He'd already been there long enough and didn't really care where they went after here, as long as it wasn't here. Two hours had passed, and they were approaching one a.m..

"How much longer you think?" Nicole asked.

"I dunno, what time did you say this place is open till?"

"Three."

"Ugh. Don't these places believe in normal operating times?"

"I think that's the point."

"It's a lousy point."

"And the crowd doesn't seem like it's waned at all yet."

"Fabulous. Could the news get any better at this point?" Bridge asked.

"Well, I guess he could slip out the back door if there was one, making us wait all this time for nothing."

"Don't even say it."

"It is possible, isn't it?"

"Remember what I told you before… there is always another door."

"Well maybe you should cover it."

"He came in through the front. As long as he feels

there's no need to escape from anyone, he should go out the same way he came in."

"What if he spotted one of us?"

"Are you just trying to think of ways to make me miserable?"

Nicole laughed. "Just want to be thorough. Trying to think of all the angles. You know, don't want you to think I'm distracted or anything." Bridge rolled his eyes as he listened. "And you can stop rolling your eyes, 'cause I know that's what you're doing."

Bridge turned his head and looked over the front seat. "You got a camera in here or something?"

"I just know you. I don't need a camera."

"Uh huh."

"If you want, I could always try to flirt my way onto the second floor. Speed things along."

"No, that's not a good idea."

"Why not? Jealous?"

"Oh, please, can we not start that again? Can we just give it a rest already?"

"Well then, why not?"

"Because he already knows you. He knows your face."

"Who said he'd be looking at my face?" Nicole knew what type of response she was likely to get, but couldn't resist the opportunity to tease her partner further.

Bridge's jaws clenched shut, trying to think of a good response before he verbalized it, not wanting to say anything stupid, or make it seem like he was mad, though he wasn't thrilled anyway. With him taking a longer time to respond, Nicole knew she had struck a nerve. She was kind of proud of it. It's what he deserved, she thought, for trying to keep her at arms length all this time they'd been together.

"You still there?"

"I'm here," Bridge said.

The angry tone in his voice told Nicole all she needed to know, but she didn't mind poking more. "Oh, you didn't respond."

"There was nothing to respond to."

"Oh. Well I said…"

"I know what you said," Bridge hurriedly replied. "He's not going to just ignore your face. You're only saying that to try and get me agitated."

"Is it working?"

"Yes! Now can we focus back on the task at hand please?"

"I'm always focused. Didn't you know that?"

As they continued bantering back and forth for the next few minutes, they finally got action. Nicole noticed Diego coming down the steps. He had a good-looking woman on each arm.

"Stop your blabbering," Nicole said. "Looks like Diego's on his way out. He's got a girl on each arm."

"Guess he wasn't kidding about liking that three-way stuff."

"Follow him on his way out, but make sure you stay back. I'll meet you there."

"How 'bout I just replace one of those girls and knock him out?"

"Nic, wait until I get there so we can double team him."

"That sounds fun."

"Get your mind out of the gutter."

Nicole got up from the table as Diego made his way out the door. She scurried over and exited as well, looking both ways up the street until she saw him again. Diego and the two girls, one blonde and one brunette, were just about to turn the corner of the building. Not wanting to lose them, Nicole started chasing after them. She passed a man who made a comment toward her.

"Hey, sweety, wanna do a little shake and bake tonight?"

Without saying a word, Nicole instantly slapped the man across the face as she kept running.

"Hey!" the man said, rubbing his cheek.

"Luke, they're going down the alley behind the building."

Bridge drove the car down the street, turning to get to the back of the building, hoping to cut Diego off before he was able to slip away. "Almost there."

Bridge slammed on his brakes as he got near the alleyway, quickly getting out of his car. He got there just in time to see Diego come out of the alley, looking like he was heading for a car. Bridge ducked down at first, not wanting his target to notice him, though Diego never looked his way. He was too busy talking and laughing with the two pretty ladies he had on his arms. As Bridge started walking toward him again, he saw Nicole emerge from the alley as well, moving a little faster than he was. She was making a beeline for Diego and reached him just before he reached his vehicle.

"Excuse me, can I cut in?" Nicole asked.

Diego smiled and started talking before he even turned around and realized who it was. "Sure, baby, there's always room for one more."

"These two gotta go though."

Diego turned around slowly, still having the woman attached to each arm. "No, I can't get rid of…" The smile quickly eroded from his face as he recognized the pretty woman he was talking to. "It's you."

Nicole gave a fake smile. "It's me."

Diego unhooked his arms from the grasps of his female companions and tried to deliver a blow to Nicole, though she was too fast for him. Before Diego was able to land his shot, Nicole gave a football style kick to the man's groin area, instantly dropping him to the ground. As Diego lay on the ground, writhing in pain and holding his jewels, one of the women, the blonde, wasn't too happy with what happened.

"All right, you two can get lost," Nicole said.

"Hey, bitch, what'd you do that for?" the blonde asked.

"Because I felt like it. You got a problem with it?"

"Yeah, I do. You just ruined my night."

"Get out of my face or I'm gonna ruin the rest of it too."

The blonde gave Nicole a little shove on the shoulder, which was definitely the wrong move. Before the woman was able to do anything else, Nicole immediately went on the offensive, closing her fist and delivering a devastating blow across the woman's face, knocking her to the ground immediately. She dropped to the ground and lay there motionless, though Nicole could tell she was still breathing. It was probably the first fight the woman had ever been in in her life, Nicole thought. Not that it was much of a fight. Nicole turned around and saw the brunette still standing there. She didn't look scared of what just happened though.

"Something you got on your mind too?" Nicole asked, ready to keep unleashing the beatdowns if it was necessary.

The brunette moved closer to her, touching Nicole's arm. "I like a girl who's a little rough."

"Beat it toots, I ain't got time for that."

The woman retreated a little, realizing that Nicole wasn't in the mood for any fun. "If you change your mind, I'll be back in the club waiting for you."

"Great, I'll be right in."

As the brunette walked back toward the club, Bridge appeared in Nicole's view. "Oh, now you show up. How nice of you to drop by."

Bridge smiled. "Well, you seemed to have everything well in hand. Why should I get in the way and mess it up?"

"I only had to step up and take control because you were late."

Bridge put his finger in the air, taking exception to her statement. "No, no, I was not late. I was right on time. I saw him come out of the alley and go to his car. I was just on my way there when I saw this… this… this superhero fly out from the alley and take on Diego and his entire clan singlehanded. It was magnificent. I've never seen anything like it."

Nicole raised her one cheekbone, giving him a sarcastic half-smile face. "Very funny."

Bridge then gave her a small golf clap. "No, I mean it, you were very impressive. You incapacitated our target, knocked out his friend, and even got an offer of some funny business afterward. That's a heck of a night's work. I applaud you."

"Are you done? 'Cause if you are, I could use your help in getting this idiot off the street."

"Oh. Yeah. I guess I could do that. If you really need me to." Nicole gave him a stern look. "I would love to help," Bridge said, not wanting to incur any more of his partner's wrath.

"What do you wanna do with him?"

"Let's bring him back to the car and take him back to the hotel."

"Are you sure that's a good idea?"

"Well we gotta take him somewhere. That's as good

a place as any. Plus we don't have access to anywhere else."

"OK. How are we gonna get him there quietly and without trouble? I'm sure he won't just come willingly."

"Don't you have something you can give him to help in that regard? Some knock-out juice or something?"

Nicole gave a devilish smile, like he was now talking her language. "Oh, I've got something that will do the trick."

20

Bridge and Nicole each had a hold of Diego's arms as they brought him through the hotel lobby. They could see the strange looks they were getting. It wasn't every day that they saw an unconscious man being paraded through the hotel. They swiftly walked to the elevator. Luckily it was late at night, or early in the morning depending on one's point of view, and the hotel wasn't packed at the time. Not that it really mattered to Bridge. He had a sufficient explanation for it. As they were waiting for the elevator, Bridge looked back and smiled at the people that were staring at them.

"Our friend here, he just can't hold his liquor."

The elevator doors opened up and the pair quickly got Diego inside, leaning him up against the side wall. As the doors started closing, Bridge looked out at the onlookers and smiled again.

"Lush," he said, shaking his head. "Just doesn't know when to stop."

Once the doors opened, Bridge threw the unconscious man over his shoulder as Nicole went over to the door to unlock it. When they got inside the room, Bridge put Diego onto a chair by the desk and propped him up against it. Bridge took his hands off the man and went over to the fridge to grab a soda. Just as he closed the refrigerator door, Diego slumped off the chair and onto the floor.

"Seriously?" Bridge said. "C'mon, dude, can't you even sit right?"

Nicole laughed. "I don't think he's got much say in the matter, Luke. Gravity is gonna take over at some point."

"Yeah, yeah."

Bridge took a few sips of his soda, seeing no reason to rush over to Diego to help him out yet, then put it down. He slowly walked over to the man and sighed, looking around the room to determine where they should put him.

"What should we do with him?"

Nicole came out of the closet with some rope. "Just sit him back in the chair so I can tie his arms in back."

"Got your favorite pair of rope I see."

"I was hoping to use this for a happier and more pleasant occasion but I guess I'll have to make do with this."

"We all have to make tough choices from time to time, don't we?"

Bridge put Diego back on the chair and held him in place as Nicole put the rope around his chest, then tied his arms in back of the chair. Once they felt the rope was tight enough, Bridge let go. He took a few steps back to see how well the ropes worked. Considering Diego stayed upright in the chair this time, Bridge figured it worked well enough.

"So how long's the knockout juice that you gave him good for?"

"Probably five or six hours," Nicole replied.

"Jesus, Nicole, I wanted him incapacitated for a little while so we could move him, not knock him out permanently."

"Oh, stop over exaggerating, he's not knocked out permanently."

"I would like to get this over with as soon as possible you know."

"Relax, I can wake him up."

"I want him to be alive after you do that."

Nicole shook her head. "I'm not gonna kill him."

"What'd you give him anyway?"

"Oh, just some of the good stuff."

Bridge closed his eyes, hesitating to even ask. "I know I shouldn't. I really know I shouldn't. But what exactly is the good stuff?"

"Oh, just my own little creation."

"Nic, we both went through the same CIA training

facilities, so we both know the kind of stuff they teach you. And judging by your results over the years, the stuff they taught me, and the stuff they taught you, is apparently completely different."

"I've never been completely satisfied with the regular stuff. That's why I've experimented with different things."

"You know what, I don't even wanna know anymore. I feel like the more I ask, the deeper down the rabbit hole we'll go with it."

"Probably a good idea." Nicole then stepped around in front of Diego. She leaned forward, then put all her might into a thunderous slap across his face.

Bridge moved his head back, not quite expecting such an awakening. "Jeez! I thought you said you weren't gonna kill him?"

"You said you wanted him to wake up. This is the best way to wake him up."

"Yeah, I said wake him up. I didn't say to knock him into another planet."

"Stop, he'll be fine." Nicole looked at Diego, who hadn't opened his eyes yet. She then delivered another slap, just as hard as the first one. She then looked back at her partner. "Well, he might have a pretty big headache."

"You think?" Bridge then looked at Diego, who still wasn't moving yet. "Hate to tell you this, but he doesn't seem like he wants to wake up. You sure you didn't use the twelve hour juice on him?"

Nicole crinkled her nose at him, like maybe she had made a mistake. "I don't think so." She then took another quick peek at their captive. "Well, maybe I did use the more powerful stuff."

Bridge rolled his eyes. "I would kind of like to talk to him before the sun comes up, Nic."

Nicole put her hand up to prevent him from talking more. "He'll be up in a minute, relax."

"I think you already said that a minute ago."

"Shut up."

"Should we both take a nap first? Maybe we can sleep in and let him make breakfast for us before we interrogate him?"

"Are you done?"

Bridge shrugged. "I guess so."

"Thankfully."

"What are you gonna try now?"

"I swear if you don't shut up I'm gonna stick something in you to knock you out along with him."

Bridge was about to say another sarcastic comment, but quickly thought better of it and closed his mouth again. Nicole then repeatedly struck Diego across the face with a bunch of smaller, less forceful slaps. It didn't seem to be working. Diego didn't move an inch.

"Wow. How long did it take you to learn this strategy."

Nicole stood up straight and looked at her partner, a stern look on her face. "One more time."

Bridge put his arms up. "Hey, I'm not criticizing

your techniques. I'm just wondering why I never learned something this effective while I was training, that's all."

"Luke, I'm warning you."

"I'm done. Carry on with your obviously brilliant procedure." He then gave her a completely fake smile, which judging by her face, she didn't appreciate. "How long did it take you to perfect this, anyway?"

"You said you were done."

"Oh, I did, didn't I? Oops. No, really, carry on. I'll just sit down and watch the show." Bridge sat down on the edge of the bed, pretending like he was about to watch a movie. "Should I warm up the popcorn first before we go any further?"

"I am warning you, Luke. Just remember that if something happens to you."

Bridge then looked at the time again. "So, uhh, when are we supposed to start questioning him again? Just curious."

Nicole sighed. "I don't understand why this isn't working. He should have woken up by now."

Bridge put his arm in the air, as if he was in school and answering a teacher's question. "Umm, excuse me, ma'am? You didn't, by chance, umm, happen to, umm, like, kill him, did you?"

"No I didn't kill him! He's obviously still breathing."

"Oh. Maybe you just put him in a six month coma then."

"Luke, will you please shut up so I can think for a minute!"

"Locking it down for one minute."

Nicole then went into her backpack and pulled out a couple more needles. She then grabbed a couple of bottles that had some type of liquid in them. Bridge didn't even know what they were. More of her special formulas probably. She then grabbed a cup and started mixing things together. When she was apparently done, she then put the mixture into the needle. Bridge had a horrified look on his face as she did the work, thinking she was going to wind up killing the man accidently. All that work they put in to grab him, and she was going to kill him. All that time he had to put up with that nonsense at the club, and it was going to come down to this. As Nicole moved closer to Diego with the finished product, Bridge started squirming.

"Uhh, what are you doing there, Nic?"

"Waking him up."

"Umm, before you do that, are you really sure that's going to work?"

"Pretty sure."

"Not a hundred percent sure?"

"Ehh, it's more like ninety percent."

"What if you're in that other ten percent?"

"Then I guess he won't wake up."

"Umm, uhh…"

"What do you want now? Do you want me to wake him up or not?"

"Well, I just want to make sure he's actually going to get up. And I don't... I'm not sure what you've got going on there, if that's going to help."

"It should."

"But..."

"Luke, would you just let me do what I need to do."

"I'm just thinking, I would hate for all that work in the club to be for nothing."

Nicole looked at him like she didn't know what he was talking about. "What work? All we did was sit there for a week."

"And you umm..."

"OK, we sat, danced, and drank. That's not work."

"Well, we were there on business."

"And did nothing important. That's not work."

"Well, I did have to go into a place that I didn't really..."

"Luke, shut up already. 'Cause if you don't let me do this now, I'm gonna shove the needle in you first to knock you out. Then I'll wake him up so I don't have to listen to you babbling all night."

"OK."

Bridge lowered his head and put his hand over his eyes. He couldn't look. It wasn't so much the part about making Diego dead, Bridge had seen a lot of dead bodies before. He was used to that part. It was the fact that he believed getting Diego to talk would make them that much closer to Rodriguez, and therefore Bill Hower. Losing Diego now would make them have to change plans. And that was something that Bridge really didn't want to do.

About twenty seconds went by and Bridge still couldn't look. He wasn't removing his hands from his eyes until he was sure what had happened. He heard a slight groan, sounding like Diego might have been waking up. Unless it was his final sounds before he croaked. Nicole looked at her partner and shook her head.

"You can look now."

Bridge kept his hands over his eyes, but split his fingers apart, so he could look through them. He noticed Diego starting to move and his eyes were open. He didn't seem like he was all the way with it yet though. Nicole made sure to change that, delivering one more, powerful slap across the man's face.

"Owww!" Diego yelled, opening his eyes fully. He tried to move his arm to put his hand on his face where the slap had just gone, but the ropes prevented him from doing that. "A little hard, don't you think?"

"Oh, I can do it a lot harder."

Diego grinned. "Sounds like a proposition."

Bridge looked up at the ceiling. "Oh my god, there's two of them." He then got off the bed and circled around to the front of Diego's chair. "Can you two get sex off your brains so we can get on with this?"

"What's to get on with, man?"

"I think we both know why we're here."

Diego tried to shrug, though he struggled to do so

through the ropes. "If you're talking about what happened the other day, sorry about that and all, but that didn't have nothing to do with me. That was all Rodriguez you know."

"I know who was in charge. That's why I need you to lead me back to him."

"You wanna get back to Rodriguez again? Man, you're crazy."

"I've been saying that for years," Nicole said.

Bridge gave her a look, then returned his attention back to Diego. "Well, unless you wanna tell me what happened to Bill Hower, then I need to meet with Rodriguez again."

"Don't know who that is."

Before Bridge could call him out on it, Nicole stepped in front of him, holding a very big needle in her hands. She seemed pretty proud of having one of that size as she held it up, making sure Diego could see it.

"You wanna change your answer?" Nicole asked. She could see by Diego's eyes, which were focused only on the needle, that he was nervous about being stuck by it. Nicole tried to play up that fear. "Now, I'm not exactly sure what the result will be if I stick this into you again. Maybe you'll live through it, maybe not. If you do, you'll be more willing to talk. If not, well then, I guess you'll be dead. Sorry in advance if it doesn't work out well."

"No, wait, wait a minute," Diego said.

"Yeah, wait, what's in that?" Bridge asked.

"Umm, I'm not sure to be honest."

"You're not sure? How can you not be sure?"

"Yeah," Diego said.

"Well I started mixing things together," Nicole replied. "Then I kind of lost track of the amounts and all, so, I'm not really sure how strong this is going to be. It might not be much, or it might kill an elephant."

Diego's eyes widened, then started blinking quickly. "Yo, you're not really gonna use that on me, are you?"

"Of course I am."

"No, wait, please. I mean, we can work something out, can't we?"

"The only thing we can work out is telling us about Rodriguez or Bill Hower," Bridge answered.

"I told you, I don't know what happened to the dude."

"No, before, you said you didn't know him."

"OK, OK, so I knew him. But the last time I saw him he was still alive. Don't know what happened to him after that. Might still be alive, might be dead, I don't really know."

"When was that last time you saw him? What was he doing?"

"He was talking with Rodriguez about something. Don't know what. I wasn't in the room."

"Who was?"

"That last time I saw him? Just him and Ricky."

"And Rodriguez never told you what they talked about?"

Diego laughed. "Are you kidding? You think Rodriguez tells us everything that he's got going on? He tells us what we need to know, that's it. Why do you think it was in private?"

"So he never mentioned anything about Hower after that meeting?"

Diego shook his head. "Not to me."

"Never mentioned, or even implied, that Hower was dead?"

"Nope."

"You still must know what kind of stuff Rodriguez and Hower were into, right? I mean, did Hower owe Rodriguez money? Did Rodriguez have some type of hold on him? Were they trying to do business together? Was Rodriguez trying to extort him? Why was a businessman from New York in bed with a man like Rodriguez?"

Diego shook his head, acting like he had no idea. Bridge had conducted enough interrogations by now, though, that he knew when someone was holding back on him. Most times in those situations, there were two reasons for it. The first was that they didn't want to implicate themselves in something. The second was, and he figured this applied in Diego's case, was that he was afraid of talking. Even though Rodriguez wasn't what one would consider a big-time player, there were still rules about how to act. And one of those rules was that you didn't talk about his business. If Rodriguez knew a person he did business with, or employed, talked about that business, that was as good as a death notice.

After waiting for close to a minute, Bridge got tired of waiting for a response. "You didn't answer the question."

"Man, there ain't nothing to answer. I don't know."

"I think you're lying. I think you do know."

"That's for Ricky to say, not me."

"Fine, lead us to him."

"There ain't nothing to lead. Man, the next time Rodriguez sees you, he's gonna put a bullet in your head before you even get your first word out."

"Well, we might just have to do something about that."

Diego knew what that meant. "If you're thinkin' that I'm gonna help you out or something, you got another thing coming. 'Cause I ain't."

"You'll do what I want you to do or else."

"You can threaten to kill me all you want. It won't do any good. 'Cause if I tell you where Rodriguez is, and he finds out, he's gonna kill me anyway."

"Maybe we can do something about that."

Diego made a face like he was crazy. "If you have me call Rodriguez for a meet, then you show up, he's gonna know it was a setup. I'm as good as dead at that point."

"He doesn't have to know it came from you."

Diego kept shaking his head. "I can't do it. I can't do it. Simple as that. I can't do it."

"You will do it. If you ever wanna get out of that chair in one piece, you're gonna do it."

"Like I said, you might as well kill me now, 'cause I ain't setting no one up."

"Listen, I don't wanna kill or hurt Rodriguez, or even you. I'm only interested in finding Bill Hower. Once that happens, I'm gone, I'm outta here. Then none of you have to see my ugly mug again."

"Wish I could help ya, man."

"You can. And you will."

"Nope."

"Let me tell you a little bit about my background. I used to do work for the government. Part of the scope of my work was in getting information out of people like you. You know what the mantra was? By any means necessary."

"Is that supposed to scare me or something?"

"No, but maybe this will."

Bridge took the phone out of his pocket and started scrolling through pictures to get to the ones he wanted. He then put the phone in front of Diego's face so he could see them.

"How do these look to you?" Bridge asked, showing Diego about twenty gruesome looking photos. "Look like something you wanna be a part of? You wanna be the next one?"

"That's all your work?"

"It is."

In truth, none of it was Bridge's work. But Diego

didn't need to know that. Bridge only needed to make him think it was. They were just the aftermath pictures of men who had been tortured as part of the interviewing process. Some were the CIA's work, some were not, but Bridge carried them with him to help with his own interviews. He couldn't say he never used a little extra muscle to help persuade someone to talk, but he never resorted to the tactics that were used in those pictures he'd just shown. All he needed to do was make people think he was willing to go that far. Once they believed he was capable, and willing, talking freely and openly usually wasn't too far behind.

"Now, the question is, how far do you wanna take it?" Bridge asked. "Because I'll be honest with you, one way or another, I'm gonna get the information that I want. The real question is, how much pain do you want to feel before you give it up. We can do it nice and easy, where you feel no pain at all, or we can do it the hard way, where you'll feel so much pain you wish you were dead. The choice is yours."

Diego closed his eyes and nodded, praying that he wasn't just delaying the torture from the man in front of him to the man he worked for if he ever found out he gave anything up. Bridge looked at Nicole and smiled.

"See? I told you he could be reasonable."

21

Bridge and Nicole were waiting across the street from the small second story apartment. They were sitting in a new rental car, one that Rodriguez wouldn't recognize from their last encounter. They hoped it wouldn't take as long for Rodriguez to show here as it did for Diego to show up at the club.

"I don't have another week in me for this," Bridge said.

"Diego said he stops by this place the same day every week. He'll be here."

"Unless good old Diego was lying."

"I got the sense he was telling the truth."

"Yeah, so did I. What'd you do with him by the way?"

Nicole shrugged. "I got him out of the way. Just like you asked."

Bridge looked at the top of the windshield, not quite

liking how she said that. "What do you mean, out of the way?"

"You said to hide him. So I did."

"And where did you do that?"

"In the closet."

"Nicely?"

"I dunno. I just shoved him in the corner and put some clothes on top of him."

"Hope he can breathe."

"He'll be fine."

"Give him the juice again?"

"Yeah. Stronger stuff this time."

Bridge's eyes widened. "Stronger stuff? Is he still going to be with us by the time we get back?"

"Relax, he'll be fine. It'll just make him sleep for a little longer, that's all. I wasn't sure how long we would be out so I wanted to make sure he wouldn't wake up for a while."

"Or at all."

"Stop. He'll be fine." Nicole then gave a brief pause as she thought about it. "Probably."

"I hope Rodriguez shows up. I'm not sure how long we can keep Diego in that room."

"Well it's not like he's gonna say anything," Nicole said with a laugh.

"I'm just talking about the cleaning people. It's not gonna look too good if they come in and discover a knocked-out man in the closet, is it?"

"I guess not. Didn't you tell them not to clean the room today?"

"Yeah, but we can't do that everyday. Eventually they're gonna have to come in."

"Maybe we can just bring him with us everywhere we go. You know, kind of like that movie, what's it called, with the dead guy? Weekend At…"

"Yeah, I know what you're talking about, and that works great in the movies. Real life? Not so much. I tend to think someone would notice."

"What's the matter? Afraid someone might get the two of you confused and not know which one of you's alive?" Nicole asked, beginning to laugh hysterically.

Bridge sat there stoically, staring out the window, shaking his head. He hoped Rodriguez showed up soon just so he wouldn't have to keep listening to his partner insult him. Thankfully, they wouldn't have to wait too much longer. After sitting for an hour, Bridge started tapping on the steering wheel, staring at the time, wishing things would speed up.

"Stop looking at the time," Nicole said. "We've got plenty of it. Diego's not gonna wake up for a few more hours.

"I just wanna get this over with."

"What's the rush?"

"The rush is I wanna get out of here and go home. That's the rush."

Nicole quickly perked up, seeing something move

across the street. "Well, looks like your wish has been granted."

"What?"

"I just saw our bird across the street. He's about to go into the building now."

Bridge anxiously looked past Nicole to look out her window. He saw Rodriguez just in time before he disappeared out of sight.

"So how much time should we give him?"

"Ehh, let's let him enjoy himself for a little while. Plus, things will go a lot smoother if we catch him with his pants down. Literally."

"Looks like we got another little problem."

"What's that?"

"Looks like we got a bodyguard setting up shop by the front door."

"That's not a problem," Bridge said.

"It's not?"

"No, it's not. You can take care of him."

"Me?!"

"Just go up to him, flirt a little, then knock him out."

"Oh, just like that. So easy."

"I agree. That's why I volunteered you."

"And what if he recognizes me from our last encounter?"

"Like I said, that's not a problem."

"How do you figure that?"

"Because I don't think he was there. I don't recognize him."

"And what if you're wrong?"

"I'm not. I never forget a face."

Nicole kept looking at the building, looking for more of Rodriguez' friends. "I don't see anybody else."

"No cars nearby with a load of people in it?"

"No, nothing. Just the one guy out front."

"Should be easy enough then."

"I'm glad you think so."

"Especially if we give him an hour. Let him get a little bored first. He won't be as alert."

"If you say so."

The hour seemed to go by excruciatingly slowly. Bridge checked the time every five minutes on the radio clock. And he said it out loud every ten minutes or so. Once sixty minutes had elapsed, Bridge was ready to fly out of the car.

"You ready?"

"Yes, thank god," Nicole replied. "If I had to listen to you repeat the time one more time I think I'd lose my mind."

The two got out of the car and started walking in separate directions. They didn't want anyone who happened by to think they were together, especially the guard across the street. Once they went down a considerable way, they both crossed the street, coming back up towards the apartment. Bridge was moving a little slower than his partner, stopping to turn his body away every time the guard looked in his direction. In truth, he didn't know if the guard would recognize either of them or not. He really couldn't remember if he was one of the ones that they got past before. He just told Nicole that he wasn't so they didn't waste time figuring out a plan. As Nicole approached the guard, she immediately started working the charm and flirting.

"Hey, cutie. What are you up to today?"

The guard could hardly believe it. The girl who rescued Bridgerton was right in front of him. "You! You're the one!" Nicole took a few steps back, realizing her cover was blown. "You're the chick that helped him escape!"

Before Nicole could turn and try to escape, the man grabbed her by the hair and started pulling her towards him. He figured he would get some extra points by dragging her up to Rodriguez. There was just one little problem with that. Bridge was right behind him.

"Hey!" Bridge yelled.

Feeling a tap on his shoulder, the man turned around, only to eat a well-placed right hand across the side of his face. The man immediately went down.

"Uhh, what happened to, "he won't recognize you, Nic? Huh?"

Bridge smiled. "I guess I was wrong."

"That's all you got to say? Really?"

"Oops."

"You knew the whole time, didn't you? That he was there. That he'd recognize me."

"Well… I mean, not the whole time. I mean, I really wasn't sure."

"So why'd you send me in there?"

"'Cause I knew it wouldn't be a problem. See! I told you it wouldn't be. We handled this no sweat."

"I'm glad you think so."

"It worked out fine. You took the front, I took the back, and here we are, nobody the worse for wear." Bridge then looked down. "Except for that guy. He looks like he's in rough shape."

Nicole gave him a sarcastic looking face. "How 'bout we go in now and stop talking out here before Rodriguez puts his pants back on?"

"Yeah, why not?" Bridge smiled, thinking everything worked out fine.

Nicole was still a little hot, though, that he intentionally sent her in knowing she'd have a problem. They went up to the second floor apartment and stood just outside the door, listening. They didn't hear anything at first.

"Hope Diego gave us the right room number," Bridge said.

"Well he's been right so far."

"True. Maybe they're sleeping it off."

Then they heard a few loud groans, both male and female. Bridge and Nicole both looked at each other and smiled.

"Isn't that nice?" Bridge said. "I almost feel bad interrupting them."

"Almost."

"Yeah, not totally."

They then looked at each other again, each waiting for the other to make the first move.

"Well, we gonna go?" Nicole asked.

"Whenever you're ready."

"I'm ready."

"So am I."

"Then let's go."

"OK."

"You wanna open the door?"

"I thought you were."

Nicole sighed, getting tired of the song and dance routine. "Luke, just open the door."

"Should I kick it in or pick the lock?"

"Try doing it the easy way first. Can you do it quietly?"

"I don't know how to kick in a door quietly."

Nicole rolled her eyes. "I thought I said the easy way? Can't you pick the lock?"

"Sure I can. But kicking down the door would be easier. Picking the lock quietly will take a few extra seconds."

"Luke, just open the door."

Bridge pointed at her and bent down to get the lock. "Gotcha."

Bridge had the lock picked in just under thirty seconds. He could have had it sooner, but he was trying to be very quiet about it and worked slower. He tried opening the door, but it only opened a little bit. There was a chain at the top of the door to prevent it from opening. Bridge took a step back to let his partner do the rest.

"Your turn."

Since the opening was narrower, Nicole was able to slide her hand through it, feeling around on the other side of the door. Once she located the chain, she slid it across, unlocking the door fully. She made sure to gently let the chain hang down to the side, not wanting it to rattle around and alert the people inside that something was wrong. They then pushed the door open and walked inside. They heard some groaning to the right of them. Bridge walked over to the bedroom as Nicole checked out the kitchen to make sure no one was there. He stood there for a minute, peeking through the partially opened door until his partner returned. Once she came back, they were ready to go in.

"You like to watch, do ya?" Nicole whispered.

Bridge sighed and shook his head, then looked at her and shook his head again. "Does it never end?" Nicole smiled and shrugged. "Are you ready?"

"Ready when you are, Chief."

Bridge lightly pushed the door open and walked in, Nicole right behind. Their hosts didn't even notice them at first. After waiting for a few seconds to get noticed, Bridge leaned up against the wall and cleared his throat. The couple in bed both jumped at hearing a strange voice in their room. Upon seeing the strangers in her apartment, the woman screamed and sat up, pulling the covers up to her neck.

"Who are you?!"

Bridge tried to quiet her by putting his hands in the air, the way a person does when they're trying to shush someone. "Calm down, calm down."

"What do you want?"

"Your boyfriend knows."

Rodriguez looked disgusted, not even caring that he was lying there in all his full glory. He lay near the edge of the bed, just looking down at the floor, wondering how he got so careless.

"I don't suppose it would do any good to yell?" Rodriguez said.

"Not much," Bridge replied.

"I suppose my guard down there…"

"Yeah, you can probably wake him up whenever you leave."

Rodriguez grinned, knowing he'd been outclassed.

"Dude, put some clothes on," Nicole said, finding his pants and tossing it to him.

Rodriguez put his pants on while he was still lying down, waiting for what was to come next. "How'd you know I was here?"

"A little birdie told us," Bridge answered. "Let's get on to the big picture. I was hired by Mary Hower, Bill's wife, to find him, since, you know, he went missing. I'm gonna do that, with or without your help. Now, this can go a whole lot easier and smoother if you do that. You help, tell me what I want to know, then I leave your life and you can get back to whatever it is you do. If you don't, then you'll probably wind up in the cemetery. It's your choice."

"So who are you anyway?"

"That wasn't one of the questions. Listen, Ricky, I have absolutely no interest in you or whatever your operations are. I'm not trying to get to anyone, I'm not trying to send anyone to jail, all I'm trying to do is find Bill Hower. That's it. Once I do that, I'm on the next plane back to the States."

"Only Bill Hower?"

"Only Bill Hower."

"How do I know I can trust and believe that?"

"Because I have all the leverage here. You're not going anywhere unless I want you to. And if I wanted more, believe me, I'd be getting more. I'm asking you, man to man, for your help. There's a woman who's missing her husband and wants to find out what happened to him. I'm only here to help in that regard."

"And if I decide to do that?"

"Then we walk out of here and we all move on with our lives," Bridge replied. "And you can get on with your booty call."

"That's seriously all you want?"

"That's all I want."

"Why'd you go through all that other jazz then? Asking around about me, coming up with the story about wanting to go into business?"

"If I just came up to you and said I wanted to talk

about Bill Hower and nothing else, would you have believed me?"

"Probably not."

"Exactly. So here we are with the song and dance."

"I'm thinking."

"Time's a wasting Ricky. If you choose not to share, we'll move on to other tactics."

"Such as?"

Bridge smiled. "You really don't wanna know." Bridge then looked at Nicole. "Should I show him my phone?"

"No, don't show him your phone," Nicole replied.

"I think I should show him my phone."

"You don't want to see his phone."

"I'm gonna show him my phone."

Bridge then got out his phone and scrolled to the pictures, which he contained in its own special folder. He then tossed the phone down on the bed, which Rodriguez instantly picked up.

"You can keep going as long as you like," Bridge said.

Rodriguez looked at about ten pictures before he put the phone back down. He didn't need to see any more. "I take it this is your handiwork?"

Bridge shrugged. "I don't like to brag."

"Yeah, I bet."

"So what's it gonna be, Ricky? Do we do things the easy way, or do I need to go get my tools?"

Rodriguez looked up at the ceiling and took a deep

breath, still not believing he was this sloppy. "Yeah, yeah, man, whatever."

"So… about Bill Hower. Where is he?"

"Beats me, man."

"Seriously? We just went through all that and that's the response you're gonna give me?"

"Hold up, man, hold up. I'm not trying to be flippant or nothing. It's just that I don't know."

Bridge looked at Nicole, thinking there had to be more. "OK, let's back this up a little. You're not denying you know him, are you?"

"Yeah, I know him."

"Well is he dead, alive, eating ice cream on the corner, what?"

"Damned if I know. I guess he's alive. At least he was the last time I saw him."

"Which was when?"

"I dunno. Couple weeks ago I guess."

Bridge sighed, feeling like there was still a communication gap. "OK, let's put this another way, 'cause I still feel like we're missing something here. What exactly was your relationship with him?"

"Just business."

"What kind of business? What did he want with you?"

"He came to me a while ago, said he wanted my help to disappear."

"Disappear? Why?"

"Said something about being investigated for tax

fraud or something. Said they were gonna find some stuff on him, things like that. To be honest, I didn't really care about any of the details. He just thought he was gonna go to jail for a long time and he didn't want to go."

"So he looked you up?"

"Yeah. Said he checked around, found out I might be able to help. So I did."

"And that's why he made those monthly payments to you? To help him disappear?"

"That's right."

"So what exactly did you do?"

"I found a helicopter pilot I knew, told him to fly him out of the country."

"To where?"

"No idea. That's where my involvement ended. Where he went after that was up to him."

"About this pilot, I heard he was into some money problems too."

Rodriguez smiled. "You're good, man, I'll give you that. Listen, the dude owed some people about a hundred grand. He was only able to come up with about fifty. I told him, give it to me, fly Hower out of the country, and you stay out too, and I'll take care of the rest. I'll start spreading the rumors about a chopper crashing, then the debt is paid in full. Nobody's looking for either of them anymore. Except for you."

"So now they both get to live new lives."

Rodriguez shrugged. "That's the plan."

Bridge went over to Nicole and whispered in her ear. "Call Eric, see if he knows anything about this."

Nicole nodded and stepped out of the room. While she was calling their FBI friend, Bridge got back to the interrogation.

"So where'd they go?"

"Couldn't tell you."

"You mean you won't."

"I mean I can't. I don't know."

"You mean, you just sent them up in the air without a destination in mind? I have a hard time believing that one."

"Look, I got a few other people involved, told them to fly the chopper to the middle of nowhere. They'd get picked up there, driven to a new location, then they'd switch cars a few more times, then get smuggled out of the country. The chopper would be taken apart so it would never be found again. I only get them to a certain point. After that, someone else takes over. That way, no one will ever know all the details. I don't know what happened after a certain point, the other people don't know what happened before it, then there's a secrecy at each leg of the journey. Nobody knows where the other team is going or where they've been. That's how it's kept a secret."

"So who'd you hand them off to?"

"Wouldn't do you any good even if I told you. And I don't mean that to be defiant or nothing. But now we're talking about people who would kill you just for asking about it. You wouldn't even get the question out of your mouth before a bullet entered your head. And that's the truth."

"How do I know all this is true?" Bridge asked. "How do I know he's not dead? Maybe you killed him. Or maybe he's right here, hiding."

"You may find this hard to believe but I don't just go around offing people. What would I kill him for? Wasn't gonna hurt me. He gave me money to do a job. I did the job. Agreement's done, we all move on."

"Maybe he's hiding here."

"Maybe he is. I wouldn't know. Listen, if you don't believe me, and you wanna torture me, have at it. 'Cause I'm telling you the truth. I can tell you just about anything I think you'll believe, but that won't make it true. What I told you is the truth."

Bridge talked to their captor for another ten minutes before Nicole finally reentered the room. Bridge wasn't about to finish until he got some kind of confirmation on what they were hearing. He assumed that confirmation was what was taking Nicole so long to get back.

"Well?" Bridge asked.

"I told Eric about this and he didn't know anything about it. So he called a contact of his with the IRS Criminal Investigation division and asked him."

"And?"

"Turns out that Bill Hower was being investigated."

"What about his wife?"

"She is not. Apparently it's only him."

"And she doesn't know?"

Nicole shrugged. "Can't say for sure. Maybe they talked about it, but maybe she doesn't know it's still active. Or maybe she doesn't know how bad it really is."

"She did say she wasn't really involved heavily in their finances. That was mostly him."

"So it all checks out so far."

"Hey, are we done yet?" Rodriguez asked.

"You're sure you don't know where he went?" Bridge asked.

"Not a clue. Your best bet is sitting on the wife and waiting for her to fly somewhere. That's when you'll find him."

"What, he's gonna contact her?"

"That was the impression I got. He kept asking how long until he got his family wherever he was."

"What'd you tell him?"

"I said, ask the people who drop you off at your final destination. They'd know better. If I had to guess, I'd say it'll be three or four years probably."

"Great."

They questioned Rodriguez for another thirty minutes, making sure that the man was telling them the truth. They got the impression that he was though. His story didn't deviate each time he told it. Both Bridge and Nicole thought he was telling them the truth. He didn't give off any of the usual clues when someone was lying to them.

"We done yet?" Rodriguez asked. "I mean, I'd like to get back to business." He then looked at his girlfriend. "I mean my business."

Bridge smiled. "Keep your priorities in place my man."

"Always."

"What do you think?" Nicole asked.

"I think we're done here," Bridge replied. "I don't think we're getting anything else and I don't think he knows anything else."

Bridge and Nicole then went to the door. Before leaving, Bridge had some parting words.

"Oh, and, uhh, tell your guy downstairs we're sorry about the whole knocking out thing."

"All part of the job," Rodriguez replied.

"You can carry on with your activities now."

"I will."

"Have fun."

"You know it."

22

Bridge and Nicole were on the flight back to the U.S.. Bridge was trying to sleep, though he wasn't having much luck with his partner talking almost the entire way home.

"I can't believe we're just gonna let it go at that."

"We're not letting it go," Bridge said. "Mrs. Hower wanted us to find out what happened to her husband. We found out."

"But we're not gonna keep following the trail?"

"Nicole, how much time do you wanna spend on this thing?"

"It's not about how much time we spend, it's about finishing the job."

"Nic, the job is finished. We know what happened to Bill Hower. He intentionally disappeared to avoid being prosecuted for tax fraud. Our job was not to bring him home. Our job was to figure out what happened. We did that."

"Just seems like there's more to do."

"There's not. Believe me, if we keep going, it could take us a year to find him. And Rodriguez was right. The people we'd be dealing with… way worse than Rodriguez. And I don't know about you, but I don't feel like putting my life in my hands for someone who intentionally disappeared."

"What if it was a child?"

"But it's not."

"What if it was?"

"Then we'd still be out there. But it's not. When we get back, I'll tell Mrs. Hower what happened. How she wants to proceed after that is up to her. But at least she'll have some peace of mind."

"What kind of peace of mind can you have knowing your husband deserted you."

"Well, I guess it depends on your point of view," Bridge said. "He was probably going away either way. One way was behind bars for ten years. He chose a different path. She'd lose him regardless."

"Just doesn't seem right."

"It's not right. Don't act like Bill Hower is some innocent victim here. He intentionally did all of this to himself. It is what it is."

"And what if Rodriguez lied? I mean, we're putting an awful lot of faith into what he told us."

"We are. But he did tell us about the IRS. We

wouldn't have known if he didn't say. That tells me he's on the up-and-up."

"That doesn't mean he was honest about everything."

"No, but I'm inclined to believe him. Besides, Rodriguez was our only lead. Hower, the pilot, the helicopter, the fake crash, it all ties together. I'm pretty sure he wasn't making all that up off the top of his head. He's not that good."

Nicole sighed. "Yeah, I know. I just wish we could've found him."

"Can't always get a base hit to get on. Sometimes you gotta take your walks."

"What's that supposed to mean?"

"It means we did our job. Did we hit a home run? No. But we hit a solid triple. And in our business, sometimes that's as good as it gets."

"I know."

Once they arrived back in New York, they drove straight to Mary Hower's house to let her know their findings. Bridge called her once they got off the plane to inform her they were coming, though he didn't give her any clues as to what they found. He hated doing that over the phone and avoided it all costs if he could. News like this was always better to say in person, he found. Especially when he had bad news. He thought it was easier for the client if they could look in his eyes, see his expressions, and know he'd done everything he could. It was harder to do that with a phone call. It made it seem like he was brushing them off and not giving his best efforts.

Upon reaching the Hower home, Mrs. Hower was standing outside the front door when her guests pulled into the driveway. She was eager to hear whatever news they had to share. But considering her husband wasn't with the pair, she assumed it wasn't of the good variety. As Bridge and Nicole entered the home, they could see on Mrs. Hower's face how worried she was. They were led into the same room as the last time they were there.

"Can I get you two something?"

"No, thank you," Bridge replied. "I'm sure you're anxious to hear about your husband."

"He's dead, isn't he?"

"Well, no, no he's not. At least, we don't believe that he is."

A little more hope showed up on Mrs. Hower's face, though she still looked a little perplexed. "Then where is he? I don't understand."

"Mrs. Hower, your husband is being investigated for tax fraud. Did you know that?"

"What?"

"It's true," Nicole said. "We've checked."

Mrs. Hower shook her head, not believing it. "I know there were some problems a few months ago, but that's all been worked out."

"Did you talk to anybody about it?"

"I talked to someone from the IRS several months ago, but I thought it was now closed."

"Unfortunately, it's still very much open," Bridge said. "Whatever your husband told you about it, he was lying."

"I don't believe it."

"We've talked with both the FBI and the IRS CI and it's true. He is still being investigated and likely would be going to jail."

Mrs. Hower looked shocked, as one would imagine a person would upon hearing such news. "I still can't believe it."

"Mrs. Hower, from everything we can piece together, your husband went down to Mexico so he could disappear. Those payments I asked you about from your bank account was him paying a man to help him with that."

"He never said anything."

"Probably because it was easier that way. You wouldn't have to lie to anybody if you didn't know."

"He just left us."

"Well, I'm not so sure about that."

"What do you mean?"

"Well, we believe he was smuggled out of Mexico and is now residing in another country. Which one is anyone's guess. There's no more trail to follow at this point so there's not much else we can do."

"Well, thank you for doing everything you have."

"I, umm, I wouldn't give up hope just yet of finding him again."

"Why not?"

"This is just a guess on my part, but he apparently made reference to one of the people smuggling him out about how long until he could see his family again."

"Oh?"

"So I would assume, and this is just a guess on my part, is that at some point in the future, and we could be talking three or four years here, is that he may try to contact you and have you meet him wherever he is."

Mrs. Hower put her hand on her face as she tried to process everything. "I see."

"Now, whether you want to wait for such a note, or whether you want to move on, or some combination of the two, that's purely up to you. And I can't guarantee that day would ever happen. I'm just telling you it's possible."

"Well thank you. I, uhh, appreciate everything you've done."

"I wish I had better news to give you."

"You gave me answers when no one else could. You've done everything I could have asked for. Thank you." Bridge nodded, then got up to leave. "Wait, I'll get you the rest of your money."

"Oh, no, thank you, but you've already given us plenty. Really. Nothing else is needed."

Mrs. Hower then gave Bridge a kiss on the cheek. "Thank you again for everything."

Bridge and Nicole then left the home and went back to their car.

"I'm bushed," Bridge said.

"Me too."

"I guess drop me off at the hotel?"

"Uhh, no, I don't think so."

"What do you mean, why not?"

"We have another contract to live up to."

"What are you talking about? We don't have any other jobs lined up right now."

"Well, I sort of offered something to someone and they accepted."

"And you didn't tell me?"

"Oh, you were there," Nicole answered. "You see, in exchange for my services, someone agreed to a massage, I think a shower, some undressing, some…"

As Nicole kept rattling off the terms of the agreement, Bridge just put his hand over his eyes. "You're not really gonna make me do that tonight are you?"

"Well… yeah."

"Awe, c'mon, Nic, I'm beat. We just had a long flight, we've been gone a couple weeks, I just wanna relax."

"And relax you shall. I'll take care of everything."

Bridge's eyes almost popped out of his head at hearing such a thing. Her taking care of everything was what he was afraid of. Something told him it was going to be a long night.

ABOUT THE AUTHOR

Mike Ryan is the author of the bestselling Silencer Series. He's also written The Cain Series, The Eliminator Series, and more, in addition to several standalone titles. He is always working on a new book, and you can be notified whenever he has a new release by signing up for his newsletter on his website at www.mikeryanbooks.com

ALSO BY MIKE RYAN

If you have enjoyed this book, you can continue on with the series by getting the next book, Past Dead, here:

Past Dead

Other Works:

The Silencer Series

The Cain Series

The Eliminator Series

The Brandon Hall Series

The Nate Thrower Series

The Ghost Series

The Cari Porter Series

A Dangerous Man

The Last Job

The Crew

Printed in Great Britain
by Amazon